OBLIVION'S

DEAL

by

Kim Kacoroski

Cover art illustrations by Kim Kacoroski, Phillipe Velasquez, and Masha Tatarintsev

Visit the author website:
http://kimkacoroski.com

ISBN: 978-1-947036-03-1 (Paperback)

Version 2017.12.03

Book Four of the Oblivion Series

Oblivion's Deal IV

Other Books in the Oblivion Series

Escape from Oblivion I

Beyond Oblivion II

Oblivion's Edge III

Flight from Oblivion V

Other Books in Flight Series

Eagle's Flight in the American Revolution II

Flight of the Ascendants in the American Revolution III

Choices from the American Revolution IV

Bridges of Flight before the American Revolution V

Testimony VI

Books in the Camelon Series

The Promise of Camelon I

The Dragons of Camelon II

History of the World According to the Druids

New Beginnings IV

Kingdom of the Golden Tara V

Introduction

*In **Oblivion's Deal**, the tune references connote perspectives that might escape the reader. The melodies sear to the heart of the matter, while dealing with inherent tensions. Music often serves to make light of a situation, no matter how grave or complex. The concept of matter is meaningless unless grounded in emotion. Researchers claim that a life without meaning is pointless. As humanity comes to terms with the circumstances of existence, it becomes important to gather the pertinent information to deal.*

Chapter One

We either work together

Or we don't work at all

Reference Tune: *One*

----U2

THE SMALL BOY rose from the floor and placed the last metal object on the towering frame. After pulling a miniature wrench and screwdriver from his back pocket, his tiny fingers deftly tightened the cone to the L-shaped brackets on the frame. Then the three-year-old child stood back to survey the rocket ship that he had constructed from the kit lay beside his feet. Marveling at the network of tiny nuts, bolts, and flat metal levers that fit together to form his rocket, he wondered where his rocket would take him, now that it was built.

People, he thought loudly to himself as he matched the structure to the picture on the cover of the box. *That's what I need now. People. This rocket looks lonely.*

He scoured the contents of the playroom for passengers.

People, he reminded himself quietly. Where could he get people? He hurried down the hallway and checked underneath his bed. Then he pulled a box from the collection of toys hidden in the dim recess. The box folded out into a makeshift fort. Groups of cowboys, horses, Indians, and cattle remained scattered among the cardboard inserts for the fort. He grabbed a fistful of plastic characters and left the opened fort by his bed. As the child hurried out of the room, he didn't notice the stealthy creature following him down the hallway. The feline had been watching the lad from his perch on the bookshelf.

The animal quietly disappeared behind the door while the boy resumed his play. Continuing to spy on the activity in the room, the creature patiently waited for an opportune moment to announce his presence. The characters the boy pulled from the fort found new life on the platform of the rocket ship. The captain of the ship was the proud chief with the headdress, his feathers signifying the success of many past flights. The Indian chief holding the staff would be the chosen one to lead the others, who came equipped with bows, arrows, and pistols. Though a motley crew, the collection inspired the boy for hours Next in line came the cowboy, ready to draw his pistol. In outer space, a person had to be ready for almost anything.

From the corner of his eye, the alert boy spotted the gray-striped tabby entering the scene. As the cat sauntered over to the latest creation of his three-year old companion, the boy rushed to protect his structure. Almost time for lift off, he didn't want any interference. His ship prepared to soar high into the heavens. A big starry sky awaited the exploration of his crew.

"Oh, no, Cat-zilla!" the boy exclaimed. Pushing his furry friend away with his assertive tiny fingers, he quickly stabilized a small plastic cowboy on the framework of the rocket. The cat looked steadily at the figure on the rocket ship that had captured the attention of his young friend while physically caving into the boy's direct hand pressure. "Away!" the boy commanded.

Not about to be displaced by a few plastic action figures, the cat stood his ground and didn't budge. Finding a small red ball lying near, the boy seized it and threw it across the floor. The cat suddenly dropped his fixation with the boy's handiwork. Escaping the gentle hand shoved against his lined fur coat, the gray creature raced for the ball like a streak of lightning. The boy watched the tabby pounce on the red ball before rolling over it with a kick. Satisfied that the cat had found another distraction, the boy retrieved a crew of plastic cowboy and Indians for his rocket. Minutes later, absorbed in his play, he didn't notice the pile of gray fur nesting over the uncovered box of miscellaneous parts and tools. Sitting snug in his favorite position supervising operations, the cat did not bother the boy for the moment.

As the cat slept, the boy listened to the chorus of birds outside. Glancing at the lush vegetation through the window, he searched for the source of the drumming. A bird with a sharp beak and golden wings made tapping sounds on a nearby tree. Like someone throwing pebbles the glass, the creature vied for the boy's attention. Oblivious to the noise, the feline stretched and yawned without opening its eyes.

Sometime in the late afternoon, the boy's father arrived home from work. After exchanging his suit and dress shoes for a white tee shirt, khakis, and bare feet, he met the boy in front of the rocket structure.

"Dad," began the boy, as he looked up at the man surveying the arrangements of parts and frozen action figures strategically placed around the rocket frame. The metal structure stood slightly taller than the child who had built it. "I need help building the helicopter. I can't figure it out."

"You found my old construction kit," his father said, amazed by the appearance of his long forgotten childhood toy. Instead of reprimanding his son for getting into his things, the man dropped to the floor beside the box cover and examined the assorted designs in the picture.

"Yes, I helped Mom clean out the attic yesterday," the boy said proudly over his discovery. Glancing at the previously worn, neglected box of metal tools and parts, complete with dozing cat, he explained," She said that you weren't using it."

The boy handed the cover over to his father so that he could see the snapshot of the assembled helicopter. Then he smoothly pushed the collection in his father's direction while being careful not to disturb Cat-zilla. The man's eyes lit up as he stretched out on the floor with several metal pieces already in his hands. Sitting cross-legged, the boy posed himself in front of his dad, and watched. He envied the direct manner with which the older man approached the helicopter's construction. It was the component to his play that had eluded him. How could he and his crew get back home if there wasn't a helicopter to pick up the floating capsule at sea? He had been studying the Apollo missions and knew all the stages of a rocket flight.

"I think that it fits together like this, Joe," the man instructed, showing the boy the assembly in his hand.

What magic! Joe thought, as his father proceeded with the construction project.

The father glanced at the small child sitting before him then built the helicopter with parts he requested from his son's small hands. He wasn't sure what to make of the tot's burgeoning interest and decided to stick with what he knew.

Joe marveled at the order created out of the mesh of silver bolts and shiny, colored, metal flats. He remembered playing with the older girl next door yesterday. She was eight-years old. Though very knowledgeable on the affairs of the world, she wasn't as skilled with her hands. Returning his attention to his father, Joe thought, *When I get bigger, I am going to put things together just like him.*

Realizing that he had spent too much time with the assembly, the man glanced at his watch and rubbed his forehead. He placed the partially assembled helicopter at Joe's feet. "You'll have to finish," he told Joe. "I gotta mow the lawn before it gets dark."

Then he rose to his feet and left.

Chapter Two

Relations with

The opposite sex

Can be sane

Reference Tune: *Never Been to Spain*

----Three Dog Night

"ONE SMALL STEP for man, a giant leap for mankind," the familiar television voice repeated.

Noticing that the builders had forgotten to put *People* in their rocket ship, Joe sensed that the playmate next to him had disconnected from the announcer's words and left him in spirit. He groped to bridge the growing distance between them. The television series about men from Mars living on a farm bored Joe, who often watched the robins tug on worms in his mother's garden. Their red-orange breasts caught his eye. They may have been able to get a man on the moon, but they lost young girls with the divisiveness of their language. He saw her back away from the television and head for the front door. Though the footage mesmerized Joe, he grimaced when he saw his older and wiser companion quickly depart. With a pained expression on his face, Joe silently edged toward her before she turned the door handle. She kept her words to herself today, allowing her actions to speak more loudly.

Joe shrugged and followed her, forsaking the distant voice on the black-and-white TV for the framework of her world.

"Wait," he pled. Beginning to mistrust the perceptions of anybody in a suit, Joe mentally compared the man to the girl. His friend, in a flimsy blouse and faded shorts, made a much better playmate. Airily turning his head in her direction, he placed one bare foot in front of the other and left with her.

The girl smiled at him as he joined her, accepting his company. Once outside and far away from the grandiose seriousness of the black-and-white TV scene, the children scampered towards the swing set. The girl sat down on one of the swings and soared for the heavens. Her high leg lifts propelled her higher and higher, while Joe shimmied up the bars of the A-frame structure until he was high enough to touch the sky. Balancing himself on the crossbar with his bare feet curled around the metal, like a bird on a telephone wire, he stood silent and dreamily watched his friend reach for the clouds. *Who needed a rocket?* She seemingly sailed happily through the air unaided by heavy machinery and the smell of rocket fuel. Once in orbit, she began to sing.

Holding the bars on the side of the swing set, he listened to the chorus and joined her after a few stanzas. His thoughts drifted with the girl's journey and the sky above, though he appeared confused by his impression. Soaring with his friend in the clouds, he looked uncomfortable and stared at the ground. Regaining his balance, images ran through his head with the frequency of the swinging friend below him. The girl soon reached his height in her motion, but it proved short-lived and she had to work hard to maintain it. Observing her swing to and fro, Joe wondered how the success of the Apollo mission would change the world. Would it affect their lighthearted world too?

Joe listened intently to his friend's song, always conveying a grounded, bright perspective on the world. Her perspective reassured him and the tense grip around the metal bars relaxed. Briefly, he gazed at the skies above, as if attempting to comprehend the universe though her vision.

Reach for stars

Return with moonbeams in a jar

Be better off than you are

Or work like a mule

Stupid and stubborn

Better stay in school

And learn how not to be a mule

Joining her in song for the first four lines, Joe orbited with the swing set. He had traveled in space before, like the time his mother made him nap in their bed for an afternoon. She had drawn the shades to darken the room. Seconds after she had closed the door, a swirl of colored dust came circling over him. He watched the speckled light display overhead and became convinced that other worlds beckoned him. Moonbeams came to him and burst into brilliance, like entrapped fireflies.

With minimal effort, Joe and his friend escaped the Earth's atmosphere for the stars and moonbeams. It had something to do with going to school, which he compared to the draft. Gone where the carefree days of hiding in the juniper bush with his silver pistol, a symbol of law and order in the West. Brandishing his shiny weapon between the leaves, he determined to deal with trouble on his own terms, or at least try. Rigid schedules, reading sessions, and spelling attempts replaced the days of free play. What ever happened to the Wild West? Not to be found in San Fernando Valley, it had come to an inconclusive draw like his life. Where have all the frontiers gone? The Wild West had been replaced by long-haired vagabonds believing that they were free, and women who were kicking their heels for liberation. His friend followed the way of the kicking women. Joe tracked her, the only person who made sense in his world. Everyday on the TV, he saw images of riots, shootings, and soldiers running around helicopters. Like the scenes depicted on the psychedelic walls at the Santa Barbara beach, he perceived the world outside his backyard in two-minute snapshots. Laced with the surrounding violence, a haze of thoughts encircled him. Those cartoons where the coyote wasted his time trying to blow up the rabbit had started to bother him and he quit watching television. Unlike his friend, he no longer laughed at the show. Maybe it had something to do with the Vietnam War, assassinations, and those news reporters in suits. He couldn't just escape into orbit like his playmate with the running commentary. Joe dealt with far more serious, Earth-bound issues.

The next day, he went to Mass with his parents and relatives at the Valley Mission. Though he really had his heart set on seeing the swallows at the San Juan Capistrano Mission, his parents ignored his request. Despite the lushness of the gardens surrounding the chapel, he could tell that children suffered at this place. Their shadows lurked underneath the dimly lit pews over the dirt floors, where miners once dug for gold. Other hints could be found in the gory stations-of-the-cross in an adobe building beside the chapel. *How could anyone pray with all that violence paraded before them?*

He recalled how he learned to jet from the scene. During a fresh spring day, his parents brought a collection of relatives with them, and the stations-of-the-cross suddenly emerged as a tourist attraction. Being six years old, he could not leave the horrific sight without reprimand. Joe casted a despairing glance at his parents. They stood several feet away and admired the display with the others. Looking out the sunny window, Joe fell into a light beam streaking across the room. The butterscotch ray cast light over the Madonna holding her stricken-dead son, and the statues faded into the brightness.

Once inside the light-beam portal, Joe met an affluent woman who wore a fancy but simple long dress. She appeared to be someone from the 1850's, the time when the Gold Rush had propelled admittance of California into the Union. The woman's hair was long and dark. She appeared to be Spanish, though he could not mistake her French heritage. A small amethyst necklace with a ruby pendant dangled around her neck.

"Where are the children?" Joe asked her. He probed the shadows for the youths in-hiding.

"The evil ones torture them," she said.

"What about the natives, the people who came before us? I saw an Indian boy underneath the Cross of Friar statue."

"It is dangerous here," she answered. "Do not linger. Otherwise you may never escape."

"It's a deal," he replied, watching the woman disappeared in the golden light of the sunbeam.

Then Joe returned to Earth, and never saw the woman again.

Chapter Three

Even if they take

All your heart and soul

You have still have to

Finish your mission

Reference Tune: *Look What You've Done*

----Bread

FORTY YEARS LATER, Joe had a job as a hardware engineer for a startup company in Silicon Valley. He had quickly pulled the company together after leaving an aerospace firm. One of their current tasks involved shielding machines from unwanted radio frequencies in the atmosphere. First, he needed more information on which frequencies to eliminate. Joe found the best resource at a university astronomy department near Maryland. Through a series of phone calls routed through the department, he finally found someone who could furnish the data he needed. Named Carrie, she worked as a research fellow specializing in planetary geomagnetic aberrations.

"You will need to account for this particular frequency," Carrie told him over the phone. "You will need a special kind of capacitor to filter out the noise. Then see what you get. It is similar to the data that we collected over the San Fernando Valley area."

"That's where I grew up," he mentioned.

"Well, did you ever experience any unusual phenomenon?" she asked.

"Only at the Valley Mission," he replied. "It was a long time ago."

"What happened?" she asked.

"Trauma-related alterations in the time dimension," he answered glibly, without listening for her response. It had been a long month in the office, and he wasn't in the mood to mince words. Being direct was his style. He knew to follow his instinct and the wandering thoughts in his head. This ability to communicate always seemed to work for him, and as a result, he found he never said the wrong thing to the wrong person. Instead, doors opened. Like digging for gold in California and hitting nothing but dirt, the lure of the hunt often determined the payback. In comparison to the miners traversing the terrain before him, Joe used his wisdom in deciding when the dirt became more valuable than gold.

Carrie took a deep breath and released a sigh. She responded, "Researchers discovered ritual abuse at the mission, beginning from its inception in the 1830's."

"Serpentines," he answered almost absentmindedly, ready to stake a claim.

"What?" Carrie questioned, making sure that she had heard Joe correctly.

"Never mind," Joe said quietly, realizing that the person on the other end of the phone paid attention. Joe knew his turf and played his cards strongly.

"Say," Carrie proposed, thinking as fast as she could. "I have a colleague who specializes in geophysics. She works in a lab at Woodsport, and she's familiar with the seismic activity in the area. She's going to a conference in San Francisco soon. Perhaps you both could touch base."

"Yes, please," Joe responded. "I'd love to meet this geophysicist. Let's keep in touch. I may be in over my head here."

"Sounds like it." Now it was her turn to provide glib replies. "Let me talk it over with my colleague, and I'll get back to you."

Immediately after Carrie hung up the phone, she called Donna.

"We have a live one here," Carrie said.

"How so?" Donna asked.

"His manner is so direct and abrupt. I can tell that he knows the world on an intimate level, and won't budge in his estimation of affairs," Carrie answered. "He speaks our language."

"Tell me more," Donna encouraged her.

"Serpentines interlaced the West Coast with these sites to exploit the Lacerta and their soul-transport system," Carrie revealed. "The Lacerta were the extraterrestrials that once inhabited the Los Angeles area. The Tangvas knew them, but the Serpentines trapped them, using them to get to the Lacerta." Then she added, "This guy is hot on the trail but doesn't know what he is up against."

"It was more damaging than exploitation," Donna asserted in her quiet manner. "The Serpentine action was beyond exploitation. Should we clue him in? Let him know the deal? Something about him seems familiar."

"I know, but I don't want to go there," Carrie admitted. "When I was a youngster, they abused me on night flights through a freight airline out of Los Angeles. That's how they kept my family in line. It was part of the network infiltrating this mission."

"Oh," Donna realized, finally understanding Carrie's deeper rationale for working with the caller, while maintaining a comfortable distance from the situation. "Joan and I will handle this one. I'll see if she wants to join me at this conference. We were a winning team at beating the riff-raff at the wedding, which took place in a southwest mission last October. Besides, Larry says that Joan likes to tag along at geophysical conferences."

"I suppose some docs need a diversion or a hobby," Carrie observed.

Donna laughed. "This man has something to say. I'll call you when we get there."

****

Several weeks later, Joan and Donna met Joe at the fountain in the middle of the mission courtyard. He recognized the women from the description Carrie had given him over the phone. Immediately, he felt attracted to both of them and waved at them from across the courtyard. They reminded him of one of his childhood friends.

"I used to come here as a boy," Joe began.

"Yeah, Carrie spent some time here too." Donna said with a sigh. "Although I think she's blocked most of it."

Joe's eyes opened wide. He moved closer to Joan, as if to confide in her. "Then my early impressions of the place are true."

"There's more to it than that," Joan admitted, surveying the grounds. She sat down on the tiled counter that surrounded the fountain. "It's safe here by the fountain. There's a portal here that provides protection from the chaotic energy elsewhere in the gardens."

"I wonder what they planted underneath," Donna commented as she sat down near Joan.

Joe quietly joined them, sitting on the other side of Joan from Donna. "Keep going," he said softly.

Without glancing at him for a response, Donna stared into the distance and began, "The early missionaries forced the Tangvas into slave labor. It constituted the revival of an old war that dated back to Atlantean times."

Joe froze at Donna's words. He continued staring into space as all the impressions flooding the consciousness of his youth surfaced. A pattern had started to emerge, and he would hang on until it had taken shape. It was like holding on to a bucking bronc. Years ago he had learned to track a tangled mesh of wires until he understood the connections. Now he tenaciously held on to the words of his new companions, waiting for the images in his head to make complete sense.

"The Tangvas were the Titan descendants of Atlas, who first governed Atlantis," Joan explained. Knowing that she captivated Joe with brief descriptions unlocking the hidden mysteries of his subconscious, she waited patiently for his cognitive abilities to put the pieces of the puzzle together.

"The Holy Roman Empire from Spain complained that the Tangvas males lacked a work ethic," Joe mentioned, recounting the history lessons of his youth.

"The Tangvas didn't want to work for the Serpentines," Joan replied.

"Where do we go from here?" Joe asked, perplexed by the omissions in his history texts.

"The Nazca lines in Mexico," Donna said.

Joe gave Joan a quizzical look. Where did Donna get her answers? She seemed to pick them out of the air.

Joan shrugged at Joe. Instead of yielding to his confusion, she intently followed Donna's track of thought with her own revelations. "They covered the Nazca lines during the Mexican War. General Winfield Scott supported the Lacerta."

"Lacerta?" Joe pondered, trying to keep up with the rapid assimilations of his new companions.

"They arrived in Atlantis after the Tangvas left for the Los Angeles area," Donna piped. "They were asked to help with the soul-transport network."

"Like the one put into place at the Nile River?" Joe questioned, begging to fuse the storyline in his head.

"Precisely," Donna said.

"This is exactly what I need to build in the hardware system," Joe surmised, relaxing for the first time during their conversation. Stretching back from the group, he precariously dangled over the water that pooled at the base of the fountain. As a hardware engineer, he was accustomed to taking the plunge and diving into any complex array of chips and wires. "We'll use this fountain as a base. Anyone care to join me for an excursion to Mexico City? A little rendezvous with the Mexican War?"

"It's a deal," Joan said, carefully weighing Donna's silent nod.

Chapter Four

The race to be the cruelest and mean
Makes those who win losers
The truth in any relationship
Is that dominance is a lie

Reference Tune: *Let It Rock*

----Kevin Rudolph

"WE DECIDED TO take a short trip to Ixtapa," Donna confessed when she called Carrie later. "We decided to ride this one out and juggle schedules." She sat down on the bed in the hotel room and waited for her friend's response. Several seconds elapsed in silence. Donna sighed, wondering whether Carrie could hear Joan conferring with Larry nearby on her cell phone. Meanwhile, Joe had gone back to his place to pack after arranging a leave of absence with the company that he owned. He planned to meet the women at the airport the following weekend. For the moment, Donna could confer with Carrie, who might provide further insight.

"Now you're talking," Carrie finally answered. "I don't mind being part of the solution. It beats staring at problems that are over my head. I'll meet you there."

"Great," Donna agreed in a soft voice. Then she added, "Joe moves quickly. He's able to follow our weaving observations, while adding a few more pertinent lines. I don't know the specifics of his project, but he appears desperate. We seem to be on the same wavelength. He senses the spiritual mission."

"Joe can help us uncover the Nazca lines. The Mexican-American War hid some of them from view." Focusing on the next step, she told Donna, "I'll e-mail you my flight itinerary and take the shuttle to the hotel. When will you arrive in Ixtapa?"

"Well, there's just a few days left at the conference," Donna replied, sensing Carrie's hesitance to comment on the California trip.

Instead of pressing Carrie on the subject, she glanced at Joan for further details. Joan recognized the concerned look on Donna's face and gave her a hurried but subdued synopsis of their developing plans, which included her husband Larry, Donna's boss Dr. McClendon. Accepting her role as intermediary, Donna lightly indulged in simultaneous conversations with both women before saying, "We have a few days to do our research and become better acquainted with Joe. He and Larry worked together on a seismic project many years ago, so he's a familiar face. We're going out with some of his coworkers from the lab tomorrow night. Joe comes highly recommended. Larry says to party on."

"So we will," Carrie agreed, with only a hint of jubilation. "I'll wait for you at the hotel."

****

Back at the office, Joe informed his girlfriend about his trip to Ixtapa. "I leave in a few days," he told her. He planted a soft kiss on her right temporal and waited for her response.

"Don't forget to check out Cozumel," Gabriella instructed him, as she handed him some information on Ixtapa. Looking at him squarely in the eye as he accepted the paperwork, she insisted, "You're bringing in the sacred feminine on this excursion."

Then she quickly swirled around in her chair and looked away, turning her back to him. Joe gently leaned over her chair and kissed her cheek as he draped his arms around her. Their small lab consisted of six cubicle mates. Though vaguely familiar with the comings and goings of each other's lives, the cubicle mates remained too reserved and focused to commit intimately on any level. Joe's covert affair with Gabriella became understated as a result. Having overheard his telephone conversations with Donna and Carrie for the past month, Gabriella secretly encouraged Joe to meet them at the mission. Besides being adept at seeing the bigger picture, as if she had orchestrated it herself, Gabriella had enough savvy never to feel threatened in any close relationship, which always seemed on her terms. Her liberating manner enabled him to pursue diverse intellectual and spiritual interests, which only added to their casual, though perpetual, romance.

"Sacred feminine?" he whispered, even though he knew the others were out of earshot. Sensing that he had stumbled upon a mystery, he asked, "Why don't you come?"

"You're doing fine on your own," she retorted, flashing her dark eyes in the atmosphere around them before facing him again.

Realizing that Gabriella had other concerns, he distanced himself. Rising from her chair, she shoved the research papers underneath his nose while he backed away. "Ixtapa is just a safe tourist town. The real consideration is Nahathl."

Hearing her pronounce the word with a heavy Mexican accent, Joe relented. With a heavy sigh, he waved the papers in the air, as if to accept his present lot in life and postpone any fiery interaction for later. He coldly stared at her. Joe sensed that Gabriella kept her reasons close to her heart, a jurisdiction where he often envisioned himself. Knowing how to leave a tender moment alone, he appeared stricken by Gabriella's hard bargain. Instead of protesting, he suddenly grinned and studied the papers in his hands. He noted that Gabriella had more than her fair share of Aztec blood, and he loved every bit of it.

"Hmmm," he began, trying to pronounce the name of the locale with the same heavy-handed accent as his partner, who apparently had seized the role of spiritual sponsor over his foray into Mexico. "The name Nahathl refers to the goddess women, who left paradise on a daily basis to bring light to the underworld called Mictlan. They represented the souls of warriors, and women who died during childbirth, which the natives considered another kind of battle."

Joe looked up from the notes that Gabriella had given him. Noticing she had left the room to have lunch with the other members their coworkers, he relaxed the tension in his shoulders and went home for the day. Sometimes silence was the best form of affection, particularly when the topic was a sensitive one. Gabriella had taught him that some things were best left unspoken, forever embedded in the realm of bodily passions for emphasis.

As he climbed inside his white Prius, he thought about the notes that Gabriella had given him for his journey. A hint of anger tugged at his thoughts. Ixtapa, the sacred site of the Aztec goddess revered for the birth of the human species, was presently own by the World Bank or International Money Fund. Although their initial goal had been to reduce poverty, it was just a thinly disguised codependency, like missionary enslavement bringing the artificial light to the heathens encapsulated in religious opiates. Only this time the Serpentines owned the bank. The connection to the ritual abuse at the mission suddenly became too clear in his head.

After parking in the driveway, he unlocked the door to his small two-bedroom home in Palo Alto. He spent a few minutes packing and slowly gathered his thoughts. His girlfriend's research remained at his side on the bed. After pausing for a brief moment of respite, he carried the notes to the bar in the kitchen and perused the information further. Then he phoned Donna.

"We need to go to Cozumel," he told her. "My girlfriend says that we must bring in the sacred feminine on our journey. Cozumel is the sacred island of the Mayan moon goddess, whom Aztecs called the nocturnal physician. Apparently the goddess's specialty was midwifery."

"You're right," Donna surmised, refusing to question his lead on the divine feminine. Unwittingly, he had made it easy for his female cohorts. It took an engineer to get to the heart of the matter without being conscientious about gender politics. Deciding to follow Carrie's preference for simplicity, Donna promised him, "I'll let the others know about the change in plans."

The phone call ended as quickly as it had begun.

****

Sensing the tension in the air, Joe and the others kept the tone of their conversation light until they finally reached the hotel in Ixtapa. They were worried about intruders or remote sensors that might thwart their mission before they discovered it themselves. They found Carrie waiting for them in the lobby. She looked up from the magazine that she had been reading and nodded in their direction. Joe could tell from her body language that she was being discrete in her actions. He shot a glance at Joan, who caught his silent message. She responded with a light shrug toward the other occupants in the lobby. Meanwhile Donna checked in at the front desk. Joe quietly waited his turn and noted the room assignments for the women, who shared a suite adjacent to his own room. Carrie quickly left the lobby before Donna and Joan followed her at a stealth distance down the hall.

After leaving the front desk, Joe entered the hall alone and climbed the stairs to his room. He saw no one in the corridor or stairwell. He turned the key in the lock and entered his room. Moments later, he detected a soft knock at the bolted door separating his suite from the women's.

"Open up," Donna said softly.

Relieved that he wouldn't be isolated from the others, he hurriedly answered Donna's knock and invited her in his room.

"Nice place you've got here, Joe," Donna facetiously cooed as she waltzed in the room like she owned the place. "Right smack in the middle of the Serpentines. I have one just like it."

"You mean *diablos*," he cued her. He didn't want to use words that might arouse suspicion in eavesdroppers. "What happened to the others?"

"They went to get tequila for some margaritas," Donna nonchalantly replied as she ushered Joe inside the living space of their adjoining suite. Joe entered the confines of the suite and relaxed in the feminine ambience. The women had lost no time in making the place their own with a few well-placed tokens from their lives at home and work. Noticing the slight drop in Joe's shoulders, Donna quickly added before he felt too comfortable, "They want us to make the nachos."

"Well, as they say," Joe replied, surveying the makeshift kitchenette as a resource for nacho fixings. Inspired by their attempt to create comfort under the circumstances, he swiftly made himself a part of the action. Following Donna's effortless hint of a jest, he wryly cautioned, "Don't drink the water." Then he paused for a few seconds before adding, "Let's get room service to bring up some chips. Skip the cheese. I don't trust dairy products this far south of the border, especially in the heart of heartless *diablo* land."

"Me too," Donna agreed as she dialed room service. She blinked and studied Joe as she spoke in broken Spanish to the clerk. Joe's play on words hadn't escaped her. He matched her seriousness with light humor, validating her choice to stay behind with him while the others foraged for tequila in the streets. She smiled at the thought of working with an engineer, they considered all the angles.

Moments later, the group gathered around a small table on the veranda outside their room. Joan and Carrie emptied the contents of their bag and began arranging glasses on the table with the precision of chemists. Donna and Joe watched them while nibbling from a bowl of tortilla chips

"No ice for me," Joe asserted, grabbing his glass and holding it close.

"Oh, that's right," Joan said, as she mixed several bottles of juice and tequila together. Without stopping her endeavor, she told the group, "Don't drink the water. Everything thing must come from a capped bottle. The last thing we need is Montezuma's revenge."

"Joe thinks of everything," Donna said to the other women.

"Takes an engineer," Carrie announced. "Now I know why you called me. You really just wanted to invite yourself to our margarita party in Ixtapa."

Joe feigned innocence, savoring his margarita, and joshed, "You're right." Then he deftly returned the party to its initial focus. As long as he made no direct references, he could openly speak about grounded historical events. He knew these groups only responded to syntax, rather than content. Halfway-closing his eyes to avoid alarming the women around him, he continued to play along, "This brings me to our burning question. Why did General Scott's men cover the Nazca lines?"

Seriously considering the direction in which Joe had steered the conversation, Carrie contented herself with a margarita from the assortment on the table before stretching out in her chair. She reflected for a moment then said, "I don't know. That's one reason we're here. We have burning questions to answer. We just decided to take a step in the right direction without wasting time deliberating our destination."

"It has something to do with the soul transport network," Joan observed, sitting down with a drink in her hand. A thought disturbed her countenance, and she immediately placed her glass down on the table before taking a sip. "The soul transport network was threatened by the Serpentine presence. They held Mexico and the western coast of the United States. General Scott worked with the Lacerta star constellation that followed the Tangvas, a population of Native Americans that emerged after the sinking of Atlantis. By the time of the Mexican-American War, the Tangvas were essentially enslaved or colonized at the mission."

"Sorta like serfdom," Donna commented as she munched on a tortilla chip. "The Holy Roman Empire simply extended its borders overseas. They wanted to seize the United States, and the result became the Civil War."

"OK, so what next?" Joe asked, abruptly changing the subject to regain the focus of their discussion.

Joan noted the man's tenacious grip on affairs and leaned back in her chair as she thought about their next move. Reaching for a tortilla chip, she groped in the far recesses of her mind for the vague answer that loomed in the shadows of her consciousness. When she felt that she had a firm grasp on the reality of the situation, she slowly sipped her margarita. Only one sip loosened her tongue. She answered Joe, "A visit to the pier is next."

Joe placed his drink on the table and quickly nodded. "I agree. That's exactly what came to mind."

Donna, sighing, immediately placed her drink down on the table, while Carrie took notice with a hint of smirk tugging at the corners of her mouth.

"Sounds like Donna also thought of the same thing at the same time," Carrie observed as she studied the contents of her glass, not quite willing to set it down yet. "We have three out of four people on the same wavelength. This is more than just a shared reality. This is serious business. Everyone, except me, perceives the same vibe, which means that I either have a block or am blocked. The real question is," she continued lightly with a calculated swirl of her margarita, "how much sobriety, if any, is required for this next mission?"

"I'll finish my margarita later," Donna decided. "The alcohol preserves well in the heat. I'm accustomed to it."

Joe set his glass down, following suit with Donna's gambit.

Carrie took another swig from her glass. "I need the anesthesia. I'm into feeling no pain. It's been a long haul just getting here. Time for a shaman's journey in a slightly altered state, courtesy of a cactus."

Joan hailed Carrie's intention with a slight sip of her drink. Then she placed it on the table with a smile. "Here, here to our intrepid traveler of inner space."

Carrie chuckled slightly as she nearly finished her drink. She'd had a head start compared to the others. Placing her nearly empty glass down, she said, "I'm gone."

Joe laughed softly as Carrie rose before the others got their feet. He relaxed slightly at her boldness, while noting her astute balance, which conveyed a sense of groundedness that emanated from within. Realizing that such a compass might come in handy, he stood next to her and motioned the other women. He acknowledged, "Let's go before it gets too dark."

For a brief moment, Joe reflected on his entourage. Donna looked to the Earth for her sense of direction; Carrie's compass flowed from her heart; whereas Joan, the wounded warrior, took her cues from the multidimensional world that soothed and enlightened her.

The group headed out the door as Joan secured the lock behind them. Together they wandered the down the streets toward the pier. Their lighthearted manner enmeshed them in the crowds inconspicuously. By the time they reached the creaky planks of the wooden pier, they were alone. Carefully walking on the wooden boards, Carrie looked up from the murky waters that appeared through the cracks and stared into the sunset. Though for the present moment she felt eternal, she knew that they didn't have much time before the darkness enveloped them and posed a mortal threat.

"They sunk a ship here," she told them. "It brought in supplies for General Scott's army."

Peering into the waves that slapped against the wooden structure that supported them, Joe said, "It was a spaceship."

Joan stared at him in astonishment. After a decidedly abrupt glance at Donna, she said, "Keep going, Joe."

"All US presidents know that the extraterrestrials represent interdimensionary souls," he told them. "It's part of their briefing."

"Yes, but the Serpentines mark them for office," Carrie added. "Like Chiron, they are wounded healers."

"Like the pharaohs, some chose to fulfill the Serpentine agenda," Joan added, recalling the folly of her namesake. Joan of Arc had been sainted by the diablos for promoting their monarch.

"We can track the Nazca lines here," Donna commented, surveying the terrain. After a short pause, she announced, "I got it. Let's get back to the room. I can map it out over a margarita."

Joan shuddered slightly, relieved that Donna had hurriedly concluded their adventure on the pier. Then she gently nudged Carrie off the dock, while Joe suddenly turned and led the way. Quietly they made their way back to the hotel. Once inside the room, Donna grabbed a pen and drew her observations on a piece of paper. Joe watched her sketch as Carrie reclined on the sofa, seemingly reflecting on life like a philosopher. Joan busied herself in the kitchenette and remained silent.

"It's a plant," Joe observed from Donna's map. "A maguey plant, a type of agave." Then he repeated the words that Gabriella sometimes said, *"Para todo mal, mezcal, y para todo bien también."*

"For everything bad, the spirit of the mezcal, and for everything good," Donna quietly translated.

"We've been drinking it," Carrie remarked, who was familiar with the different types of liquor traded with the culture south of the border. "The bottle of spirits used tonight contained a worm, which means that the brew is mezcal rather than tequila."

Joan curiously looked up from the glasses that she had been washing. "What did Gabriella mean, Joe?"

Joe hesitated to answer, preferring to allow another woman to fathom the depths of his lover's reasoning. Gabriella had instructed him to pursue the divine feminine during his travels, and he figured that he could use all the help he could get from his female cohorts. Unlike most men, he didn't mind asking for directions once he could admit that he became lost. Sometimes he reveled in his wanderings, because he learned more that way. Something about the ability to let go and give up control over the outcome made life interesting. Maybe because it was life, rather than some prepared, freeze-dried experience, which some substituted for the real thing with all the artificial contrivances of a modern society. He liked to keep his edge. Rich or poor, he liked to keep his fingers on the pulse of life, often opting for earthy, simple, functional designs rather than dysfunctional, cold, overdone arrangements. There was a time to keep up appearances and a time to do what mattered, such as breezing through life without going to extremes.

"A motto for our times," Carrie confessed, contentedly closing her eyes and dozing off.

"They covered the Nazca lines with dirt. As they were unable to make out the runway, this preventing the Gray's spaceships from landing," Joe surmised, refusing to comment on the meaning of Carrie's words. Unlike most men, he knew when he was over his head. His motto: "Never question a mystery when it appears. Just sit back and enjoy it, rather than answer everything, and in the end, to everyone. Instead start by answering to yourself." In this manner, he asserted mastery over his own life rather than pursuing perpetual puzzles. Paradoxically this described how he obtained his best answers. He simply placed them within the eye of the beholder. Perhaps this was why the women around him always seem to accept him.

"It was another intergalactic war," Joan asserted, contemplating her words in the historical context. The implications were mind-boggling. This time she chose to bring a glass of water to her lips. "It involved another time wrinkle. President Polk got caught in it. General Scott got him out and seized the advantage."

"That's how we won the Mexican-American War," Joe claimed.

"I'm ready for Cozumel tomorrow," Joan said with a sigh. She didn't want to dwell in the density of such a heavy subject, particularly south of the border where chaos reigned. "We gotta keep moving."

Joe heard her and nodded. "I'm off. Time for me to call it a night." He left Donna's side, and headed towards the door connecting their suites. Before closing the door behind him, he swung around with a light cheerful wave, "See ya tomorrow, *amigas*."

"*Si, si*," Donna cried excitedly as she put her map away. Joe's winning manner swayed her to suddenly drop her work and prepare for tomorrow. There was more to know, another adventure in the making.

****

The next day the group hurriedly packed and hopped a plane to Cozumel.

"This is the place," Joan observed when they had reached their destination. She had kept her reservations about their quick departure to herself, because wasn't sure whether they had gathered all the information that they needed in Ixtapa. Yet the fast-paced motion of their travel proved revealing in itself. They weren't meant to dwell in the three-dimensional world of a grade-school history lesson. Like an airborne craft, their mission was to simply skim the surface of previously known realities and connect the dots. They could fill in the emerging patterns with details and color later. Collectively they looked around for further clues regarding the inter-dimensional story of the Mexican-American War. Sandy beaches and rippling blue water loomed in the distance. The sight of the waves affected Donna immediately, as if it had specifically conveyed a thought to her mind. Perceiving the message, she shouldered her bag with a subtle conjecture, "We gotta hit the Mayan ruins."

With the air of a sea captain, Joan raised her head in the breeze. After a moment's pause, she proposed, "Let's drop these bags at the hotel first. I want to be light on my feet."

Joe lightly grinned and shook his head, admiring the way his cohorts found a needle in a haystack. He wondered what sort of encounter awaited them at the Mayan ruins. Without further hesitation, Donna hurried toward the hotel that they had booked early that morning. The rest followed her.

Once they reached their hotel rooms, Donna dropped her bag and studied the tourist maps. She seemed to be tracking the same frequency that the rippling waves had brought from the beach. Joe placed his bag in the suite next door before joining Donna. He examined the assortment of maps surrounding her, then asked, "Where to next?"

"We gotta take a jeep to Castillo Real," Donna proposed.

Joan looked over her shoulder. "You're right. It's a watchtower."

"Not just any watchtower," Carrie announced. "It guarded the sunken Atlantean crystal from alien discovery."

"Figures," Donna said. She wondered sometimes where Carrie got her information, especially the details that resonated with her own soul. Though Donna felt alone at times, there was always Carrie and her inclusive ways that seemed to envelope her in a giant grand unified theory, which some scientists called GUTS. Now Donna realized how much GUTS that Carrie's mental ventures required. Donna felt that she herself just went beyond the given reality, whereas Carrie's trajectories eventually amounted to a complete orbital escape.

Joe shrugged at Joan. "This particular watchtower is where I can find the frequency model for my computer design. A few capacitors should settle it out."

Joan raised her brow at his words. She still did not know exactly what Joe did for a living. So far he had remained rather vague about his projects. Trusting her instincts, she had entertained his presence on their journey. Now she knew that it wasn't just a show. Joe's technical expertise provided a wired schematic for all of their metaphysical endeavors.

"I detect a portal in the area," Joan reported, pointing her finger at a space in the picture. "It's for dwarves."

"You're right," Carrie remarked. "They have a message about the appropriate use of technology."

Meanwhile, Donna had already started dialing for jeep excursions to the site. Minutes later they boarded a shuttle at the entrance of the hotel. The shuttle took them to a crowded parking lot where they could join the next group going to the watchtower. The caravan of vehicles bounced over short, bumpy roads that seemed to go nowhere. The passengers quieted during the ride as their eyes hungrily scanned the horizon for signs of rippling blue waves.

After the driver stopped at the site, Donna hopped out of the jeep behind Joan. They dispersed in the area, going their separate ways from the rest of the tourists. An overwhelming sense of curiosity drew each of them to various places. When they finally met each other near the base of the tower, the foursome spoke in hushed voices.

"Somebody gridded the watchtower with the Glastonbury Tor and Lia Fial," Donna noted in amazement.

"Not only that," Carrie added, "but they cloaked the area in diamond dust. The dust has its own particular frequency."

"There's my frequency," Joe said excitedly.

"Hush," Donna cautioned them. "This tour is crawling with Serpentines waiting for the innocent to reveal their discoveries. Make like you're bored and head back to the jeep."

Joan looked around, suddenly feigning an immediate yawn. Then she turned and walked alone to the jeep. The others shook their heads before following her. After at least another half-hour, the rest of the tourists returned to the jeeps. They chatted animatedly while the foursome kept their detached silence during the drive back. Once they returned to the hotel room, their mood switched quickly.

"Next stop is the Arizona-California border," Carrie announced as they gathered around the coffee table with cups of green tea.

Without questioning her, Donna punched the keys on her laptop to determine the exact spot. Finding the location that matched her own sense of direction, she admitted, "I sensed that Arizona would be the next place, too. This means our gridding here is done. Time to skedaddle. Tracing the lines of energy along the border, I come up with Yuma, Arizona."

"Me too," Joe softly echoed as he walked slowly toward the women.

Carrie and Donna looked at each other and then at Joe, who approached them like a thousand-year-old friend. Visibly moved by the realization that he was on the same wavelength with his counterparts, Joe allowed his countenance to relax. Joan gently put her hand on Joe's shoulder. Nodding at the Donna and Carrie, Joan told them, "We have third-party verification here. Yuma it is. The next question is why Yuma?"

Donna took a deep breath and explained, "From the what I recently experienced south of the border regarding the California mission, it's obvious that Spanish royalty pursued this portion of the continent for Serpentine operations."

"In other words," Carrie continued, "the Mexican-American War sufficed as a thinly disguised alien invasion."

"Yuma it is," Joe said with a sigh. This time he walked away from the women to collect his thoughts on the veranda that overlooked the beach. He purposely had used the present tense in last statement and needed time to adjust to the sound of it.

Joan thoughtfully watched him leave. Deciding not to spend too much time figuring the man out, she leaned over Donna's shoulder and studied the area around Yuma. "Well, it isn't exactly Roswell, but we get the picture."

Out of the corner of her eye, Joan noticed Joe wince at her strategically placed words. She observed that Donna had also seen his reaction, while Carrie sensed it with a slight shudder before tossing the sensation off her shoulders. Spending a few seconds to compose herself after the shock, Carrie blinked before beaming wryly at Joan. Joan almost smiled when she caught Carrie's mischievous sense of adventure, which reminded her that there was nothing like watching the previously doomed have a good time. Carrie, who had suffered enough trauma during her last visit to the missions to never want to attend church again, seemed more than willing to brave an out-of-this-world encounter, provided it proved fruitful.

****

The next day they landed in Yuma and took a cab straight to the Colorado River on the edge of town. Casually separating and pursuing different directions along the river's edge, they shouldered their bags and collectively explored the area. Joe strolled to a mesquite tree. Relishing the shade underneath it, he dropped his duffle bag to the sandy desert floor and thought a moment. The military managed a base nearby, which prohibited lengthy inquiries. The river flowed swiftly and deeply in front of him. Allowing his thoughts to drift with its current, he played the frequency of the Cozumel diamond dust layer in his head. It didn't match the airwaves in the region, which puzzled him. Carefully he picked up a small stone and skipped it across the river. Joe found his answer in the action of the stone crossing the water. The density of the water layer shielded the extraterrestrials from discovery. They continued to operate right underneath the noses of the Gray's base next door without being detected. The Anasazi had cleverly left this establishment in another dimension long before the Serpentines invaded the Dragon flyer bases of the Aztecs.

Carrie strolled toward him from a yucca a few yards away. She surprised him with her observant words. She seemed to see right inside him. "Got the frequency that you need?"

"Why yes," he told her, stepping away to study Carrie more closely.

"Great," she responded with a thoughtful stare into the distant current. "Let's get out of here. The air is too heavy with military eyes."

"Eye in the sky," Joan commented as she joined them. "We are being watched."

Donna waved lightly at them as she trudged through the taller grass in front of them. She smiled at them as if nothing could ever be askew in her world. "Let's get out of here," she said.

Checking in a hotel less than a half-mile down the road, they gathered in Joe's room this time. Though the feminine invasion surprised him, he refused to call attention to it. The women had accepted him, and Joe now perceived them as allies, especially since they could get on his wavelength and speak his own thoughts. Their boldness was reassuring, as well as endearing. Carrie glanced at the electronic schematics that he had been drawing. An abrupt nod betrayed her understanding. Immediately she turned away. Noticing Carrie's reaction, Joe realized how much she knew. This time it was Carrie's turn to take a thoughtful stroll outside on the veranda. Donna's eyes tracked Carrie's response. Facing Joe, she glanced at his drawings.

"We have another time wrinkle on our hands," Donna surmised, interrupting the silence.

"It concerns the Philadelphia Experiment," he confessed. "It really happened. This place confirms it."

"Let me guess," Carrie speculated while returning to the room. The wispy curtains bellowed behind her as the desert wind picked up momentum over the sparkling lights of the city. "You were burned by the government."

"That's only some of the raw deal. It is not over, especially for the bulk of humanity. Whatever the military wants, the military gets," he admitted sadly, shaking his head. "My present experience of this country differs from what I had learned about the American Revolution during grade-school history classes. Instead, my education in the corporate world taught me that the Serpentine-driven military took over the nation after assassinating Lincoln."

"So now you are working at a tame, startup company," Joan observed.

"How did you guess?"

"You have too much time on your hands for a hardware engineer," Joan told him. "You're slaking."

"Not really," Joe replied, refusing to reveal himself further. "I respect my earned freedom. I just don't want to work like a slave or corporate serf. True wealth is being able to do what you want and do it how you want. It has nothing to do with money. Sometimes it is just a feat of engineering, where you play with the rules of physics to manifest the divine intention."

"I believe you," Carrie said as she slumped down on the adjacent couch. "You're not a slacker. Now, about that time wrinkle from the Mexican-American War..."

"President Polk got caught in the time wrinkle, and General Scott pulled him out," Joe replied. "Several members of the Romanov family were in Mexico aiding Quartermaster Thomas Sydney Jesup, the unsung hero of the Mexican-American War. His mother Ann O'Neill descended from Irish chieftains. Many nations were involved, choosing sides in this war that almost erupted into Armageddon."

Hearing his explanation, a painful thought crossed Carrie's mind. Without spending time trying to figure things out further, she blew a short, soft whistle. "Let's leave early. I don't want to disrupt the present-time continuum."

"Agreed," Joan said, giving a Carrie short hug before leaving the room to retire for the night.

Although she didn't fully understand Carrie's reasoning, Joan provided additional support for Carrie's motion with a decisive departure out the door. Her years dealing with life-and-death issues in the medical world had taught her all about timely endings, as well as untimely ones. Seasoned, she wasted no time or words going for the finish.

Without further discussion, the remaining women left Joe alone in the room. As he watched them leave, he offered a feeble wave. Crestfallen, he became aware that his heart wasn't in his work. Carrie's revelation had provided the one factor that he had overlooked---personal peril. He felt grateful that the physicist had spelled it out for him in so many words. Before disappearing from his sight, Donna chuckled lightly at him. Her light manner reassured Joe, and he broke out in an uneasy grin. Satisfied that the tension had been broken, Donna turned on her heels, following Carrie out the door. She assured Joe, "All's well that ends well."

****

As they left early the following morning, the group kept their conversation light. Together they returned to California, where they would go their separate ways for the next month. Everyone needed time to assimilate their discoveries in the Southwest. A quietness hung over the group like the solitude of the desert. No one wanted to press the issues that they had touched lightly, preferring to stay with superficial reflections rather than plummeting murky depths.

Joe waved the women off to avoid detection in a public place. He turned and headed for the parking garage where he had left his vehicle. The three women watched him quietly disappear in the crowd. Then Joan and

Donna arranged a direct flight back to Massachusetts, while Carrie waited at the airport for another plane going to Rhode Island. She wanted to confer with researchers associated with the observatory before returning to the astronomy department. Located at the university, the observatory had a collection of astronomical clocks that could be used to calibrate time wrinkles.

"It won't be the last time we hear from him," Joan told Donna as they hurried to catch their flight.

"Joe's here to stay," Donna estimated. "He knows he's in deep. I saw the look on his face when we first landed in Ixtapa. I was afraid that he was going to faint and that I'd have to catch him."

"Yes, he is sensitive," Joan said with admiration. "He picks up on the subtle energies like a radio receiver."

"He keeps his cards close to him too," Donna remarked. "He's on his own."

"Given the information we gathered on our trip, that's probably the best thing to do. He's not alone anymore."

"No, I suppose not," Donna replied. "Neither are we. It's a win-win situation. We both picked up another ally. Carrie says that he's been doing some interesting wiretapping on the military-government. She saw his schematics. He really has been burned."

"That's what concerns me more than anything else," Joan confessed. "He is playing hardball, though I suppose it's one way to get information, especially if the military-government tapped him or tried to kill him. The rest of us just run. This guy deals."

"Deal us in," Donna quipped as they joined the crowd boarding the plane. "I could use a breather."

Chapter Five

There is comfort

In attaining a view

Of tomorrow

Reference Tune: *The Morning After*

----Maureen McGovern

JOE DROVE HOME from the airport. After entering his house, he left his bags at the door and walked to the computer workstation near the kitchen. Joe turned on the computer so that it would start processing while he resumed settling in his home. Keeping a neat house, he delighted in the play of efficiency and organization in his life. He operated like a refined ballerina, always sneaking in a subtle, graceful lilt following a timed arabesque. Joe constructed his life on those lilts, which served as a trademark and betrayed his sense of spirit. He never took the time to look for a reflection. Instead, he intently focused on matching his precision with the synchronous way events moved around him. The day he quit elegantly lilting his way through life's rhythms would be the day his heart stopped beating. He didn't just build a machine---he pursued designs that were sleek and proficient. The lilt was like putting a signature on a creative work and taking ownership of his life rather than mindlessly laboring through it. He always looked for the angle, the artful perspective that could do wonderful things like demand play out of drudgery.

Once he had settled in his home, Joe turned his attention to his wiretapping project. Learning that his enemies tapped his work and home, any wiretapping existed as a two-way street. He could either cloak or manipulate his information. Those on the other end weren't aware that he could see them. In their eyes he represented another victim. From Joe's standpoint, he merely leveled the playing field, making the situation transparent.

He looked up the operations in Yuma, and learned that they were related to the Philadelphia Experiment. During World War II, the US Navy decided to conduct experiments in time travel, invisibility, and teleporting. The military-industrial-complex existed long before Eisenhower had labeled it that in the 1950's. From the beginning, the US military had been intertwined with commercial interests. American revolutionaries bought gunpowder from the same French company that later operated Alexander Hamilton's bank. Even though the royal French funders of the American Revolution had been beheaded, the British avoided attacking the French gunpowder factory in the War of 1812. The gunpowder factory had been a logical target for the British, but unholy alliances dictated military maneuvers. In World War II, the Allies never bombed IG Farben for reasons known only to the military. Following Eisenhower's admission of the military-industrial complex, there had been three incidents of boats and sailors lost in time wrinkles. One of them involved John F. Kennedy's PT boat. Those involved created a cover story for the five sailors missing in action, except this particular action pertained to illicit naval operations rather than enemy fire. As with the Battle of the Bulge, the motive not only had been genocide but also purposeful elimination of those who knew too much, common in a war that ended through the questionable use of technology. In his wanderings through military documents, Joe had found the listings of those men targeted in the Pacific. The group included the top frogman who could have singlehandedly ended World War II in his mission. Set up by his own government, the frogman met a knife to the heart when he climbed on board the Japanese vessel. Who betrayed him? Who really had called the shots in the war? Joe could only guess. The recent trips had brought him one step closer to the answer, and several steps closer in the design of his latest innovation, one that would make him millions of dollars.

Reflecting on his project, Joe added a few more variables to his integral calculus equations. Some of them incorporated the frequency of the diamond dust layer found over the Yucatan Peninsula. With a few taps on his computer buttons, he had his solutions. All he had to do know was figure out the capacitance and ground the network correctly. He sat back in his chair, crossing his arms over his head. Joe detected another presence in the room. She always came when he had found the correct venue for their joint venture.

This time she shimmered at the threshold between his workstation in the kitchen and living room. She wore a long purple gown that appeared translucent white in the glow of the afterlife. Her auburn hair fell gracefully on her shoulders, while her eyes stared through him into the distance; he could never remember their color. The vision of her dazzled its way into his thoughts like a whisper in the wind.

"What did you see?" she asked.

"Where?" he questioned her.

"During your latest travels."

Joe dropped his arms to his side as he sat back in his chair. Blinking a few times to be sure of the correctness of his sight, he responded, "You. I saw you floating in the diamond layer."

"You're right," she acknowledged with a wry grin, aware of her sparkling translucence and making the most of it. "Am I transparent now?"

"Very," he admitted with a hard swallow, noting the contours of flesh underneath the gown.

She moved toward him. The closer she came, the more she pulled Joe out of himself. The structures of all his thought paradigms always disappeared in her presence, until he felt light and free. He rose from his chair to hold her in his arms. Wishing to touch and feel her next to him, Joe found that her warmth soothed and refreshed him. Nuzzling his right ear with the heat of her lips, he heard her silent words. She didn't need to speak out loud anymore. It wasted precious time in their moments together. He merged with her translucence until he left his body for hers. Somewhere in another dimension he found a timeless unity with her, a place that spoke to his depths and called him forward. *You are the divine feminine, an interdimensional being*, he told her without speaking.

She responded with a dewy kiss on his lips, confirming his suspicions. *I'm on the right track*, he thought when he soared with her through endless time, entering a vortex so complete that he hungered for nothing more.

"See me," she urged him as the intensity of their fervor escalated.

Closing his eyes, Joe drifted into a heavy sleep. The woman instantaneously moved him into a relaxed, blissful state. He felt her lie down next to him. Slowly he revived after seeing the light. This beautiful woman had removed the bitterness from his soul, ejecting the lancing betrayal of his own government.

His own story returned to him unblemished by emotional judgment. Feeling her fragrance envelope him like a sweet flower, Joe recounted his final days working on a project with a large aerospace corporation. One by one, the people in his office had been removed by a series of tragic circumstances, sometimes appearing self-inflicted. A colleague had been laid off; another had relocated; one office mate had died in a freak car wreck; and their team manager suddenly had developed cancer. As Joe reflected on these circumstances, he noticed the woman begin to disappear.

"Wait. Stay until I figure this out," he pled. "I want wholeness. I need to reconnect with these important parts---you, me, myself, or whatever it is that I don't know."

She looked seriously at him with her light-green eyes, the ones that always saw through him. Now as she vanished, he remembered the color of her eyes and kept this memory alive. Seeing past the silvery mist hanging around her form, Joe connected with the distant look in her eyes. Her body trembled as he sought her, but she did not blink or move. Instead she faded away under his stare, leaving Joe with only her heavy gaze as remembrance. Shutting his eyes, he took her inside him. When he opened them a few seconds later, the interdimensional woman was gone.

"You're right," he thought out loud. Joe rubbed his hand over his right temple. Then he shook his head before lowering his hands back to his laptop. Tossing off the density of his recent revelation with his thoughts, he spoke to the ambience of the past encounter with the interdimensional woman, "It is heavy. Keep looking up. Got it."

Joe's fingers flew over the keyboard as he toyed with a few more designs and equations in his head. After couple of hours, he felt content with his answer. He shut down the computer and hopped from his chair to retrieve the rest of his bags from the front door. He had purposely left them unattended, as if they were variables in another integration, one that he had saved when he had tidied other seemingly loose ends. After some light unpacking, he decided to cook some dinner before retiring.

He hurried to bed so that he could get sufficient rest for an early rise. There were a few things he needed to do before his coworkers arrived at the lab tomorrow morning. After sensing the inevitable at the aerospace job, he had left a few devices in the computers they once had paid him to build. The signals from the devices could be picked up with his machines in the lab. There were many ways to wiretap---mentally, energetically, and electronically. He was accomplished at all three, and it hadn't been difficult. His corporate enemies had been so focused on his undoing that they had forgotten about their own peril. He had realized their wrongdoing early in the game they played. Maintaining his silence, Joe had gotten out quickly before the company noticed his absence.

****

The next morning, he slipped out of the house and drove to work as the sun rose over the valley. Joe relished seeing the city after it fell asleep. It gave him a different perspective on the illicit affairs that ran the business of government. Other times he watched in amazement as the valley slowly erupted into its crowded, harried life like an oozing volcano. Cruising around the town prior to the bustle left him with the eerie feeling that he was above it all. He never intended to get caught in such a mindless existence, especially when so many things happening under the surface of a contrived reality. Although his perspective had been by choice, occasionally he wondered whether it was a delusion or a ride in a hot air balloon. He scrutinized his observations, figuring he owed it to himself to tell the truth, even if he seemed the only one listening. Despite being under no obligation to let anyone else in on his secrets, he never made any attempt to hide what he learned to be true. The price for his knowledge had come at an incredibly high price, which represented part of the deal.

For the moment, Joe contented himself with enjoying the ride. Truth would always surface, regardless whether he pursued it. Besides, he could always phone Carrie if he needed a reality check. Apparently, she also had suffered more than her fair share of revelations, ones that she could not ignore. At some point an individual was forced to choose between truth and insanity. Fortunately, Carrie had chosen to find the truth before the other issue ever arose.

As the first of the sun's rays peaked over the eastern horizon, Joe recalled the woman who had entered his dreams last night. Her vague presence had reassured his soul that he could entertain illusion safely. She was teaching him how to fly, how to make his dreams real. As Joe recalled his reflections of the previous evening, he parked his vehicle in the vacant lot. Stepping outside of the delusion that haunted the sleepy town, he turned the key in the locked door to the office, flipped on the lights, and got to work.

Oh, it's you, Ms. Dorothy Kilgallen! Joe greeted the machine instead of the woman. In his silent thoughts, he chose to ignore the apparition posted next to it. The computer appeared more alive to his consciousness, sometimes conveying the stilled voice in a lighter, more workable reality. Without turning to face her, he acknowledged, "What's my line?"

"You know you must maintain silence," she replied with wink as Joe checked his notes.

"I know," he said with a sigh as he typed the keys furiously.

Chapter Six

The emotional reality

Is that you can't be saved by love

Reference Tune: *Operator*

----Jim Croce

SHIMMERING IN THE hazy sunlight, the woman by the computer told Joe, "There's another level of understanding. What are you finding in the research concerning your former company?"

Joe reflected for a moment before turning her question around. "It's not like the investigations that you've done. You must have known that there would be repercussions for your journalistic research concerning Roswell and Jack Ruby's Carousel Club."

"Nothing like what happened," Dorothy insisted with a light toss of her head. She never suspected that they would murder her and then systematically destroy her public image as a result of her investigations. Her viewers had known her by her phrase *what's my line*, which died with her.

"So now are you the patron saint of those who find that they know too much?"

Dorothy squirmed a little in her seated position on the computer table. Readjusting herself for balance, she pressed him. "I'm not the only one on the other side trying to get critical information across. You're just the only one listening."

Joe paused for a moment and thought about her statement. "Comes with the territory."

"The more that you know, the more you are held responsible," she observed. "On the other hand, ignorance is not blessed. A person may fear what they are about to learn, but the ignorant might as well be dead."

"It's a life," Joe painfully confessed, recalling the zombies that would be rising to get to work in a couple of hours. Then he turned and faced her. "What did you learn?"

"That you have it," she stated. She saw the look on Joe's face as he considered those existing in sombalistic lives, which weren't worth the effort. "Gossip is another distraction from the truth, that we all must deal with sooner or later. Joe, you have meaning."

"True," he admitted.

"Don't shut me out."

"I'll pay attention," Joe bargained, unwilling to make a commitment. He shrugged his shoulders at the gossip. Lowering his head to focus on his word, Joe made it clear that he preferred minding his own business, even if she had something truthful to say. Joe's friend, Tobias, had cautioned him that malicious gossip constituted a form of modern-day witchcraft, because it destroyed lives and communities.

"All right," Dorothy acquiesced.

"The problem with the last job is that they wanted me to design a system that could handle backdoor spyware," he explained. "Initially their proposed project irritated my moral fiber. Later it scared me. Who would want to do such a thing? And why? Curiosity replaced my fears. When I exited the company, I left the backdoor open on the project. I needed to substantiate the rumors so that I could anticipate their next moves and save myself, perhaps even a few others like me."

"On many multidimensional levels," she added. "You turned the tables on them. Now you are the spy on Big Brother."

"Student," he corrected her. "I'm not a journalist. It is different. I'm not so cocky about it, because I know that my efforts could get me killed, which is the difference between you and me. This educational research might be the one thing that saves my life, which is why you're able to access me. I admired your work as a journalist, so I hear you. I am always surprised to find that I am the only one paying attention, and astounded by what I learn. Life is full of surprises---that I do know for sure."

"Let's get on with it," she said. "You found something important this morning. I sensed it, which is why I'm here. I can guide you through this."

"Help is always appreciated," he told her. "I can find my own way, though." Joe continued to study the data on the machine before consulting the journalist on the other side. "It is just as I suspected. They hired someone else to do their bidding. The military pushed for this project so that they could not only manipulate electronic data but also spy on anyone or group. Now they want to use the backdoor technology to sync every car computer to the operation of their choosing. What happens if they decide to interfere with the function of the steering wheel?"

"There's a bigger picture," Dorothy said, examining her fingernails in slight boredom.

"It has to do with your investigations on the Grays and Roswell," Joe ventured.

"Yes." Her presence glimmered brightly for a few seconds, and she began to disappear. Instead of holding steadfast in her position, she told him, "Now you're on track.

"Dorothy, you're fading on me," Joe accused her. He watched the woman sitting on the table vanish, but he decided to confront her before she left. "The problem doesn't pertain to Roswell. It exists at Yuma."

"That's my line," she murmured. Only her voice remained in the air. "Now you know more than me."

"That's not funny, Dorothy," Joe replied. Noting the absence of any echo in his thoughts, he relaxed in his chair. Satisfied, he reveled in the silence and his ability to chase away a spirit with his revelations. He called it "spooking a spook." Lately, it had become a pastime. With so much information on this multidimensional subject from the deceased, he had to protect himself. They all had their own opinions and emotional debris. Dorothy proved one of the more direct ones, so he entertained her longer than the others. The deeper he delved into this extraterrestrial topic, the more polluted became the airwaves of thought, as well as his two-way tapping endeavors. He never pursued them. Good and bad, they found him, and it was his chosen task to deal, rolling with the punches. Nonetheless, he remained fairly ruthless in the manner with which he sifted the information, though their appearance implied tacit permission. His life depended on it, and providing assistance was their chosen karma. He always would continue to question them. Having deviated from the truth once, they might do it again. Clarity proved paramount.

Now that Dorothy had disappeared, Joe decided to consult a human being rather than take advice from a disgruntled spirit. Like wiretapping, this endeavor also worked as a two-way street. He decided to give Joan a call before the other office mates arrived and overheard their conversation.

"Quick question," Joe started when he heard Joan answer the line. "What did the Anasazi have to do with the Grays?"

"Skip the Grays, Joe," Joan answered. "Look at the Serpentines."

"You're right," Joe replied after he thought about her answer. The Grays reflected the aliens instigating the confederate rebellion after the Mexican-American War. The Serpentines maintained Lucifer's ambitions. Unlike Dorothy, Joe felt that Joan could almost anticipate his reasoning, which served as another reality check for him. He appreciated the well-intended intervention. "The Anasazi ran protection for the planet."

"Yes," she said breathlessly, sensing that something was amiss in the analysis. "I need more time to process this information. This seems more complicated than I initially thought. I'll check with Carrie. She might have an angle on it because of the time wrinkle."

"I know," he agreed. "That's why I called. Thanks for humoring me."

Hearing Joan's light chuckle on the other end, he patiently waited for the disconnecting click. Then he hung up, relieved that he wasn't the only one who needed time and space to think about the implications.

Joe greeted his office mates as they came in through the day. Gabriella had gone on vacation during his absence, so it would be another week before his could indulge her with stories of the divine feminine south of the border. She would have even more to say about her own travels, offering a depth of perception that Joe never grew tired of seeing through her eyes. Like Gabriella, he held a major share in the company with several partners. Tonight, Joe stayed later than the others to tie several loose ends together that were related to his main business.

Missing rush hour traffic, Joe drove home in the setting sun. By the time he stepped inside the front door of his home, he found himself in the dark. Pausing briefly to stare into the void, he wondered in amazement at the sight of nothingness. This familiar, reassuring feeling often surprised him with certain clarity. The exercise momentarily turned his gaze inward, then his eyes adjusted to the varying lighted hues streaming in the room. He traced the illumined streaks to various sources. Streetlights, stars, and moon interrupted the stilled darkness. Noticing a shiny, sparkling figure at the far end of the room, he curiously looked at the sight.

The woman in the purple dress shimmered in the dusky hue near his workstation. "Wait for Carrie's call," she instructed. "You need help spiritualizing the information. She can direct you."

"Thanks," Joe murmured as he wandered across the kitchen. He flipped on the dim LED lights over his desk, wishing not to disturb his vision with too much brightness. "I'll call my friend Tobias first. It's the place to start before Carrie takes me into the stratosphere."

The woman nodded. Joe imagined kissing her softly on the lips before dialing Tobias's number.

"Hey Tobias, tell me about hydrogen," he began when his friend answered.

"Hydrogen is about beginnings," Tobias told him. "It's the parent of all elements. It's primordial."

"Keep going."

"Hydrogen pertains to the conflict between matter and spirit."

"Oh, I see," Joe said thoughtfully, placing his feet on the table as he leaned back in his chair. "It brings us to solid-state physics."

"You got it. Go for it."

With those final words, Joe said goodbye to his friend in Oregon, who worked as a naturopathic physician. They had met while kayaking the San Juan Islands off the coast of Washington. Joe had cut his hand on the metal rudder, while Tobias happened to be paddling nearby. Like a shark, Tobias arrived as quickly as the blood began to drip off Joe's palm. Offering homeopathic arnica, calendula ointment, and butterfly bandages, Tobias saved Joe a trip to the emergency room.

Joe hung up the receiver and waited patiently for Carrie's call.

"I heard that you were onto something," she greeted him a few minutes later. "Joan asked me to call you."

"Tell me about solid-state physics," Joe said with slight hesitation. He wasn't sure what kind of answer to expect from Carrie. "First let me skype you in," he said. "I want to be able to see your face, so that I can tell when you are joking or leading me astray."

"Me!" Carrie protested, but Joe would not take no for an answer. Though she relented, he suspected that she wouldn't let him off easily. Her face appeared on his lap top screen within moments. Seeing a wry grin tug at her lips, Joe knew that she would seriously entertain him. "The reality about solid-state physics is that nothing is solid," she said.

Joe slightly nodded and let out a sigh. "Okay, you lost me, but I'm hanging on by my fingernails. Keep going."

"Reconsider those basic physics classes of yesteryear," she teased him. "Remember the task of measuring bond distances between atomic particles. Theoretically, your desk is nothing more but fast-moving particles separated by space. You should be able to slice your hand through it."

Joe touched the top of the table before him. He hit solid wood. Then he admitted with the hint of a tease, "I'll have to work that one out."

Carrie giggled a little. With a twinkle in her eye, she said, "Larry is teaching Joan how to break bricks with her hand."

"Hmm, she did mention that she had married her martial arts instructor," Joe observed, grateful that Carrie had given him a piece of information that he could visualize in concrete terms. "Go ahead. I'm with you."

"Here's your next question," Carrie pushed further. "How does a charged particle gain energy?"

"Let's see, Einstein," he joshed. Now he felt he was on solid ground. "It takes a changing magnetic field or an electric field to accelerate a charged particle." He deliberately slapped his hand on the desk. "Physics---those were the days, my friend."

"I bet you thought they'd never end," she added.

"Keep singing," he said.

Remember the subtle geomagnetic anomalies at Yuma?" Carrie asked. "The Anasazi shielded themselves from Serpentine infiltration with a hydrogen-based fluctuating magnetic field."

Joe whistled softly. "The river ran through it. They used the hydrogen atoms of the water molecules."

"The water literally served as current," she summarized. "Water is the primordial element."

"I've heard this somewhere before," Joe mused. Then he repeated his earlier conversation with Tobias, "Hydrogen pertains to the division between spirit and matter."

"The Serpentines are only interested in matter, because they lack a true spirit. They exist only as illumined matter, superficial reflections like those found off the water's surface."

"They only see themselves," Joe commented.

"The perception must remain skin deep or else they vanish. It's the reason for all the smoke-and-mirror devices," Carrie responded. "The question remains...do they constitute another inertial system? If they do comprise an inertial system, the laws of physics would be invariant, according to special relativity."

"The Serpentines have no light of their own," Joe reasoned. "Beneath the smoke and mirrors, the laws of physics will vary."

"It is like making your own rules," Carrie commented.

"Whew!" Joe heaved, almost breathlessly. "I need to sleep on this information before we go any further."

"Yeah, me too," she agreed. "I guess there's a lot more to it. The Serpentines are hiding something in the Rocky Mountains, and that is the reason they want people out of Colorado Springs, even if it means torching neighborhoods. Yuma is just a tributary to them."

Ending their discussion with this last point, they said goodbye quickly. Joe hurried to bed after pursuing this angle in his investigation. Early the next morning, he received another call from Joan. Taking advantage of the three-hour time difference between the east and west coast, Joan wanted to catch Joe before he went to work. They had become familiar with each other's habits from their travels together. Joe and Joan had often risen before the others and talked while they sipped herb tea during the sunrise.

"Donna studied the seismic activity concerning Yuma, Yellowstone, and Mount Saint Helens," Joan explained. "She and Larry expect an eruption in Yellowstone within the next two years."

"How's Carrie?" Joe interrupted. "I stayed up late doing more research. They are hiding human trafficking beneath the Rockies. It is the same organization operating the missions."

"They must be the Blues," Joan surmised. "Carrie told me that she had a difficult night last night. How did could you tell?"

"The Blues are the alien group that employs mind control," Joe added. "The Blues destroy the mind, whereas the Grays annihilate the body. The Serpentines tap into the spirit. Your former stalker, Nicholas runs the Grays. A cardinal in northern Italy controls the Blues."

"Makes sense," Joan remarked. "Carrie did mention the cardinal once. Do you think she was earmarked for the Blues' program underneath the Rockies?"

"Yes. I think she was the fish that got away. She's hot and they try to pull her into hospitals to see what she knows about the operation. In their minds, she's still the subject in an experiment."

"She's safe from them now," Joan speculated. "She's figured out how to elude them."

Chapter Seven

The best time to take a bath

Is when you've hit bottom

Reference Tune: *Take Me To The River*

----Talking Heads

JOE AND JOAN continued their discussion for a few more minutes. After both agreeing that they needed more time to consider the deeper implications and relationships, they ended the conversation. Tapping into the information on his former company, Joe sought the connection between Yuma, Yellowstone, and Mount Saint Helens. Within minutes he had his answer. Then he drove into work and called Donna from a secure line in a private office.

"They are digging a tunnel between Mount Saint Helens and Yellowstone. Can you check on it from a geologic perspective?" he asked.

"I'll check on the geologic data in those regions," she replied. "If there is a tunnel, the concentration of research may reflect the location. These days most regions are surveyed according to economic incentives. No one does it for academic purposes anymore, much less aesthetics."

"Yes, I know how the money drives scientific inquiry, which is why we must contend with so many illusions." Joe acknowledged. Then he suggested, "Can you check on Carrie? I think that she knows more than she realizes."

"I'll ask her over for dinner tonight," Donna decided. "She can relate with those who get kidnapped by the Blues, like she still remembers the same wavelength or something. She even connected with those trying to escape the shootings at Columbine school."

"I see," Joe responded. "They may be linked. Whatever the Blues learn from the experiments goes mainstream. I think that is why all those vampire books do so well through Internet manipulations on social media."

"Maybe that is why Carrie always seems to be ahead of the mind-control game," Donna reasoned. "She has already built up her immunity."

"Could be," Joe observed. "E-mail me at home tonight. My lines may be tapped. I am in the process of changing to a different provider."

Later in the evening, Joe received an e-mail from Donna while he was puzzling over his electronics schematics. The words flashing across his screen surprised him. She had kept it brief.

"Carrie recalls being taken to Saint Louis during night flights when she was between four and six years old. During the Vietnam War, fighter pilots from a local airline company practiced combat skills on groups of children. Those who passed were abducted to Yuma and fed into the Blue's system."

Joe wrote back, "This brings us back to the missions."

Donna replied, "It looks like the next volcanic eruption will be in Yellowstone. Carrie suspects the programming is done closer to burned region in Colorado, whereas most of the trafficked children are housed at the Canadian-Wyoming border. Whatever blows near Yellowstone probably will seal the underground exits. Like you, Carrie has a wireless two-way tap going. She says that we need to let the trapped experiment subjects go. It is an act of mercy."

Joe leaned back in his chair with a soft whistle. After a reflecting for a few moments, he typed another question. "Did they ever catch Nicholas, the vampire who stalked Joan?"

Donna replied, "Joan e-mailed me fifteen minutes ago. They caught Nicholas in a sting operation while the president of the United States visited a billionaire from a prominent software company."

Joe said with a low whistle, "One down. Only the cardinal is left of the deadly duo. Spiritual predation remains. There may be retaliation. I'll contact my friend Tobias about more protection and get back to you."

"Thanks," Donna wrote back.

Moments later, the inter-dimensional woman appeared next to Joe's workstation. Taking a break from his typing, Joe munched on a light snack consisting of soup and a sandwich. As he leaned back in his chair and sipped on green tea, he recognized her form.

"There's more to know," she told him with vibratory shimmer that ran through her entire body. "A time wrinkle in India inspired the American Revolution."

"Oh," Joe replied, rubbing his head while he placed his feet on the desk. "I never would have guessed. Are we talking about a colonial version of the Philadelphia Experiment?"

"Hundreds of people disappeared in India. They targeted the spiritual elite. Only a dozen were lost in the Philadelphia Experiment."

"I see," Joe said, still rubbing his head. Bewildered by the enormity of the crisis, he observed, "Calcutta never recovered." Looking at the clock, he added, "If the population ever got around to dealing with the past, they could redeem themselves."

The woman nodded in reply. She stared fixedly at Joe as her countenance brightened. The vibration filled the entire room with a pale blue light. The vibration calmed and reassured Joe, who yawned suddenly.

Transfixed by the display of color, Joe's manner softened. Shutting down his computer, he rose and backed away from his desk. With a sense of reverence, he promised, "Let me sleep on it."

Chapter Eight

The world always accepts lovers
Maybe not technology or science
The future exists for those
With social skills

Reference Tune: *As Time Goes By*
----Rudy Vallee

THE NEXT MORNING, Joe returned to his office. Alone in the building, the early morning shadows amplified the death-like atmosphere. He walked over to his wiretapping device and entered a few key words. His thoughts searched for another link with Dorothy Kilgallen. He wondered whether she was present in the same room or busy someplace else on the planet. Within seconds, Joe found his answer. The familiar three-dimensional image instantly appeared. She sat perched on his desk with one leg dangling impatiently in front of him.

"What did you find out about the PT boat blindsided by the Philadelphia Experiment?" he asked her, not wishing to waste any words.

"Thought you'd never asked," she retorted. "The incident is the Rosetta Stone to the McCarthy hearings and UFO phenomenon."

"You were behind the times," Joe reminded her, as he leaned over his computer without giving her the benefit of a glance. He didn't want to be distracted and make the same mistakes she had. His life and livelihood depended on his ability to maintain focus.

"I paid for that steep learning curve," she mused as a slight shudder ran up her spine. "Too much gossip and too little analysis of the information."

"Tell me more, Dorothy," Joe encouraged, refusing to look up from his computer. Her past efforts had obviously proved unproductive. Besides wishing to avoid the same whirlpool of intrigue that had drowned Dorothy, he wanted to give her some space. Instead of playing her game, Joe confronted her, "What do I need to know here? My first priority is to stay alive."

"Right," she stammered as she rearranged the priority of thoughts in her head. "They intended to kill everyone on the PT Boat."

"That must have complicated their experiment," Joe reasoned. "Most experimental scientists don't include murder in their theories."

"It did mess up the experiment, but only in the conclusion," observed Dorothy. "There were survivors who lived to tell the tale. Shelly Winters lost some close friends on the boat. She helped carry their souls across."

"Let's stick to the present," Joe requested. "It is never a great idea to kill off the scientists in an experiment. What were they thinking?"

"Power and money," Dorothy remarked with a sigh. "It is an old story."

"What else were they trying to hide?" Joe questioned her. "Sounds like this is just the tip of the iceberg."

"It is," Dorothy replied softly. "Only those on the other side see it, though."

"Will I have to wait?"

"No, I'll fill you in, but only because you are listening and obviously willing to entertain a few spirits."

"It's my sixth sense," he insisted. "Comes with the electronics."

"It's all about mind control. Keep your sixth sense. It's your best defense."

"Mental pirates?" Joe quizzed her.

"Pirating the mind, which beguiled me."

"Manipulated?"

"They brought in aliens through the time wrinkle," Dorothy said. "Like the ones at Area 51. Fortunately, the aliens died in the passage. They dumped the bodies at Area 51 for further study."

"From what I gather with the two-way tapping, McArthur used extraterrestrial help in the Pacific," Joe told her. "He must have known about the aliens trying to come through."

"That's why the military-industrial complex stopped him from winning the war and restoring peace to Asia. However, after the botch time-wrinkle experiments, it became a free-for-all," Dorothy elaborated. "The extraterrestrials who helped McArthur were souls in other dimensions. He observed some of the aliens picking up the soldiers who had been killed. Some men missing from the PT Boat collision with the Philadelphia Experiment were identified with the extraterrestrials. Kennedy could still communicate with them. He used a language based on numbers."

"That's heavy," Joe concluded.

"It gets worse," Dorothy interjected. "The assassination in Dallas constituted a near-alien abduction. The Grays wanted to take over the Pentagon."

"Did they succeed?" Joe asked.

"Partially. The roses in the limo served as a portal."

"What do they want?"

"Those who funded the atom bomb and Philadelphia Experiment want planetary destruction. They feed off traumatized souls," she told him. "The others, like the Grays, just want a job or a life without meaning. It's not about the money."

"Such as a job in TFX missile construction?" Joe pressed her.

"Admiral Byrd had the mistaken impression that it would lead to enlightenment," Dorothy explained. "He ran into some Grays while on an expedition in the Arctic, but the contacts appeared as a reflection of his own soul. He over-identified with it."

"Sounds like the people running the smoke and mirrors are the biggest fools," Joe observed.

"True, but they are deadly," Dorothy said with a quiver. "The Serpentines play everyone against each other. JFK would have lived if his cousins had not betrayed him."

"Like Hegel's dialectic?" Joe asked.

"They funded Hegel's research, too," she quipped. "Enough for now. I'm beginning to fade."

"Me too," Joe agreed. "It is a lot to think about. I suppose alien abduction is another name for soul annihilation."

"It is a concern, but so far the only souls obliterated have been their own," Dorothy recognized. "Carrie turned the tables on them with her time wrinkle."

"There's hope," Joe surmised as he watched the woman nod and slowly disappear.

Chapter Nine

There is nothing like a complicated love affair
To help you find yourself

Reference Tune: *Foolish Games*

----Jewel

THE NEXT DAY, Joe rode his ten-speed bicycle to work. As he switched gears, he sensed that something inside him also had shifted. Pedaling in the early dawn over empty roads and past vacant office parks, he wondered about how Gabriella would respond to him when she returned from her vacation. Would she be perceptive enough to notice how he had returned to his former self? He had reclaimed the man before his rapid exit with the aerospace company. Putting pedal to the medal always centered him. It was as if he had fallen back on himself. Never having been one to spiral down after an unfortunate event, Joe always caught his own free falls in the heart beneath his own chest. Would he find Gabriella still there after their hiatus?

More than just a minor tug-of-war pertaining to Gabriella, bigger, more pressing questions remained and occupied his thoughts---hows, whens, wheres, and ifs concerning world events and affairs. Nagging question about Dorothy Kilgallen and the role her appearance played in his life concerned him now.

As he locked his bicycle at the bike rack outside the entrance to the building, Joe realized heaven held no space for gossips. Dorothy communicated with him to work through karma. She had to come clean with information on her past journalistic pursuits, especially now that she had a different perspective. He pressed the buttons on the security lock and walked into the building. Placing his bike bag on the desk where Dorothy usually sat, he mentally searched the room for her presence.

"So what served as the spiritual motivation for JFK's passing to the other side?" he asked as her form took shape in front of him.

"He retrieved the missing men in the time wrinkle," she answered with a shrug. "The five who disappeared were declared Missing In Action. Other human beings tagged with him through the time wrinkle. They souls came from a time wrinkle in India, shortly before the American Revolution."

"When the Pluto ley lines hit Dallas, it became time to go," Joe commented. "An astrologer told me that."

"Overdue," Dorothy responded. "JFK cheated fate. They played songs from the Rat Pack on the PT boat. One of songs spoke to his soul. Luckily, he hung on to it."

"Which song?" he asked.

"The whispers behind the veil say *As Time Goes By*," Dorothy replied.

"That song is enough to make time stand still," Joe commented. "Modern day financial gurus place people ahead of money and things. Physics is more concerned with things, whereas metaphysics concerns *beings*."

"Apparently the song did the trick," Dorothy said with a slightly bewildered toss of her head. "The missing souls became the impetus for a major Hollywood cover-up. Then McCarthy put them all in a crucible. However, you must remember who funded Hegel and his hack job on metaphysics. Hegel's sponsors had to do something after the time wrinkle in the 1700's, and their plans carried over to the next century. They started with the philosophical infiltration in France prior to the French Revolution, where they turned the population against the intellect. It served as the Holy Roman Empire's first successful experiment in mind control."

"So that became the game," Joe reflected. "There were deeper issues than communism."

"Communism proved a superficial hoax," she added. "Remember, the intention is to play both sides against each other. Properly funded, Hegel and Marx turned the dynamic into a philosophy. Unlike the East-West concept of balance in their philosophy, the intention is to unhinge the collective consciousness through constant strife."

An odd thought flickered across Joe's countenance. He reexamined his notes from a previous tap. The world's end game was beginning to make sense.

"Tell me about Ghandi," he said pointedly.

"He joined the subterfuge," Dorothy quipped.

"Which subterfuge?"

"The US assassinations of the 1960s," Dorothy replied. "They killed Ghandi as part of the cover-up and made him look like a martyr. Those who commit the murders are as vulnerable as those who carry out the murders."

"What murder did Ghandi commit?" he asked.

"This lawyer delivered India into the hands of the corporate oligarchy," she told him. "The Grays controlled India through the Brahmins and *nadas*. After the Lincoln assassination, occultists assumed national power. Ghandi studied underneath Tolstoy. Tolstoy represented a self-professed anarchist in the czar's court, the same royal family who had helped blockade the British trading companies during the American Civil War. The *nadas* systematically placed their foot soldiers in the Pentagon, which carried out the intergalactic order to kill those who didn't play. As with the Nazi operations, foot soldiers obey orders without question, especially when their pockets are lined with various promotions. They anticipated an emerging vulnerability in the 1960's, and killed all the Ghandis to hide the evidence. JKF and RFK attempted to take advantage of the weak link in the system, but they were out-numbered. It's in Jaqueline's tapes, which she placed in a time capsule."

"There's more to the story," Joe realized. "Ghandi paved the way for the East India Company to nest all the electronic money in Kochi, India, which had been headquarters for the Old World spice trade."

"MLK became bitter, though he had enough *soul* and connections to make a bad idea like martyrdom look good," Dorothy continued, ignoring Joe. She had more information to convey. "Nobody could tell which way he would eventually swing. Would he sell out with his hard-won freedom? He probably didn't know until JFK's funeral, where he watched the military intentionally drop the casket. Then he knew the score. The Ghandis fooled everyone, except those who dealt with them. Battle lines were being drawn in World War II. Nobody recognized their enemies on until the Philadelphia Experiment landed on top of them."

Joe shuddered. "I imagine that it took longer than that in other parts of the world."

Dorothy glanced at Joe and quietly nodded. After taking a deep breath, Joe double-checked his notes. Then he said, "So a significant portion of the world pays homage to intergalactic powers that want to destroy the planet. Now we are talking about the Vatican ratline extending an olive branch from the Serpentines to the Grays. It was created for the Lincoln assassination and stayed in place for the Kennedys---which made it predictable. An occultist like Nostradamus could be easily misplaced as a prophet with a timely revision occurring in 1947 and 1961. It is sort like the occultists infiltrating the French parlors in time for the French Revolution and War of 1812."

"Don't forget the Ottoman Wars, which led into WWI," Dorothy added with a callous shrug. "WWI also was carried out for the corporate empires. Remember General Smudley's Book *War Is a Racket*?"

"The real war came in WWII," Joe commented.

"Those who flew for the Allies during WWI were buying time," Dorothy corrected. "That war wasn't a complete wash of dirty money,"

"Time for what?" Joe asked.

"To buy time to prevent genocide. DNA diversity---the key to survival of the human race."

"What other kinds of races are there?"

"You'd be surprised," she said with a nervous laugh.

"You mean that it is more than just *men are from Mars and women are from Venus*?" he taunted.

"In the beginning," she started, "we were all celestials. Some split off and began to lose their light, eventually fading into dark. They became parasites on those who chose the light. When the light beings refused entry, a war broke out and the illumined ones retreated. They employed technology to promote their existence. After the destruction of a series of key bases, Earth was created as a device to elude the dark forces. Initially it protected the celestials against the Serpentines, but Serpentine infiltration caused some of the celestials to decay into Blues and Grays."

"There's more," he said while checking the tap. "You've only told me what I have pieced together from my research and common knowledge."

Dorothy shrugged, sidestepping Joe's remark, "I don't know them all, but distinct groups of celestials evolved over time in different star systems. There are Arcturians from Arcturus. Pleiadians from the Pleiades cluster. Lacertas from Lacerta, and many others."

Joe stopped for a few moments to think about the implications then resumed his work. He merely replied, "It makes sense. The Serpentines are trying to kill all the celestials and manipulate all the hybrids."

"That's the shortest summary that I've ever heard," Dorothy quipped.

"It comes with the schematics," he confessed. "Brevity is my passion."

"When does Gabriella return?" she asked, changing the subject again.

"How did you know about Gabriella?"

Dorothy watched him at work for a second. Then she politely said, "Never mind."

Joe smiled to himself. The lively art of turning women off always served him well. He enjoyed being selective, especially when it came to spirits. Interdimensional lovers were another matter. He appreciated his privacy and the fact that Dorothy would now respect it. It served as her lesson and his task to teach it to her. Somewhere in the heavens, they had forged this contract. Meanwhile, they enjoyed the exchange of information; she told him everything he needed to know concerning the tap, and he pieced it together for her. As a marriage made in heaven, and nowhere else, the deal forged a temporary arrangement. Joe turned and watched Dorothy fade before his eyes as he finished the tap.

In the evening, he took Gabriella out to a local winery for dinner. As the sun set over the distant hills, he relaxed in the billowy orange-gold of the sun rays. Unlike Dorothy, Gabriella appeared quiet and more reflective, which he appreciated. Tonight, however, he noticed that his lover seemed quieter than usual. Something weighed on her mind. Joe determined to fish for it and baited his hook.

Gabriella beat him to it. Sensing his thoughts, she abruptly turned the tables as she intently forked through her refried beans. "Did you find the divine feminine during your travel?"

Taken aback, Joe folded his arms across his chest and eyed his companion. He should have known that she would have only one thing on her mind, bringing in the divine feminine. Experience had taught Joe to be cautious when it came to other people's projects, especially when unsure of his own contribution and value in the investment. Then Gabriella flashed her dark eyes at him, and he melted under her intensity. Dropping his arms, he slightly shrugged and replied, "Well, yeah."

"Good," Gabriella insisted with an air of passion. Satisfied that she had disarmed him, she turned her attention to her plate and tugged on a soft tortilla with her fingers. "*Bueno*."

Joe changed the subject. "Would you like a glass of wine?"

"Anything but the stuff down the street," she said. "My girlfriends are telling me that they've infused it with a drop of human blood."

Joe smirked a little with a quizzical tug at his lips. Though she had caused him to drop his guard, Gabriella had nicely offered herself, or what she thought was herself. He never ceased to admire her sense of decency, but it wasn't what he wanted. Joe had been fishing for Gabriella's thoughts. Instead she gave him the divine feminine and several other women to boot.

Joe, however, refused to give up. Having seen too much of the darker side of life, he feigned innocence. Instead he continued to play, and told her with a deadpan look, "Well, isn't that just a satanic thing to do? Imagine that. Next thing you know, we'll all be addicts."

Chapter Ten

Is it legal?

To walk away from love

Reference Tune: *Touch Me In The Morning*

----Diana Ross

GABRIELLA QUIETED when she heard his words. Joe could tell that she didn't know whether to laugh or cry. He had come clean with her without giving himself away. Now all she had to do was decide whether she wanted him, while he waited and pondered their destiny. The wheel of fortune had brought them together again.

A moment of silence passed between them as she stared at her plate with a softer vision. Joe silently nodded at her for a second and then looked away. He couldn't bear it anymore. He didn't want to hear anymore, and he searched for the exit. Divine feminine or not, Joe could not---would not---be taken. Rising from his chair, Joe left and quickly paid their bill at the entrance before Gabriella uttered another word. Luckily, they had taken separate cars. Now he knew why.

Joe stepped inside his car and angrily jerked the steering wheel around so that the car swerved out of the parking lot. Turning the corner like a race car driver, he sped down the road, far away from Gabriella. His travels with the three women had given him a taste of intimacy that he couldn't get out of his mind. Gabriella had fallen short somehow.

Calm down, my boy, Joe told himself, as if he was talking to a small child. He knew his temper well and realized that it had the potential to fall on himself, missing his heart at times. Joe felt angry at himself for suggesting dinner and attempting to make meaningful conversation with someone who had another agenda. Gabriella had tried to rope Joe into politics instead of romance. If he didn't watch it, he might direct this rage against himself, and there would be no end of it. He would hear it, and he would be the only one, the sole individual to fathom the depths of his angst and painful understanding. He wasn't sure he wanted to go there. Hot tears pulled at the corners of his eyes as he stared into the blinding rays of the setting sun. His sunglasses had lost their ability to reduce the glare. He sighed in frustration as he lowered the shade with a harsh, quiet tap of a semi-fist. Even if he had a reason, he had better talk to his inner rebel before he lost control. Whether or not she knew it, Gabriella had set off a minefield inside his body.

Realizing that he didn't really want to go home, Joe relaxed and drove straight for the beach. He didn't want to hear the messages that Gabriella would leave, trying to bandage a wound that required stitching. He didn't want to hear it anymore---the standard laments, the subtle accusations, the "Why don't you do..." More than anything else, Joe valued his freedom and his desire to have a quiet mind, even if he had to do the peacemaking himself. Only a handful of people seemed to have a grasp of the undertaking.

Arriving at the surf almost an hour before midnight, Joe left his car parked on the bluff and skated down the steep, sandy incline past the community of coastal sage scrub. Though he couldn't see the beach waves, he could hear the pounding of the surf calling to him, inviting him in like a mother. A familiar bond with the sea made him to smile despite himself. He was here to play, here to be loved, and here to bask in the beauty of the night.

Remembering to take off his shoes, Joe raced to the source of the noise that deafened his ears. He didn't have to lend his ears anymore, opting to cloak himself in the thick, salty mists exuding from the never-ending white froth. Tearing off his shirt before rolling up the hem of his slacks, Joe left his clothes and shoes in a pile he could easily be retrieved. Always the cautious one, he designed his life like a safety engineer; he always felt he had a lot to lose. These little details that touched him were highly valued, because they reached into his soul and exposed him to himself, the one person that he knew would understand.

Heading for the surf in the hazy light of a waxing moon, he scanned the horizon as he waded in the froth. Several silver human forms shimmered on the surface. They seemed to be waving to get his attention. As the miniature tides unfolded around his planted feet, his consciousness connected to their beautiful souls. Their fishtails appeared to beat with the rhythm of their thoughts.

Go back to Gabriella, they told him as he felt his defenses drop. *She's desperately trying to pick your brain, and she wants to be allowed in. Take no offense. You must take that woman in your arms. Get her out of her head. It's the only way you'll quiet the echo of your thoughts.*

If he hadn't felt so relaxed and refreshed by the salt air, Joe would have discounted the advice coming from these half-fish people. Instead he leaned over his toes and scooped some of the water with his hands. He wiped his face with the moisture left in his hands. Then he peered into the shadows that danced in the moonlight. Nothing had changed after this hygienic ritual. The silver merpeople were there, still waving joyfully at him. Realizing he would have missed them if they had disappeared during the two seconds in which he closed his eyes, Joe dismissed his rebuttal.

"Thanks for the vote of confidence," he responded. "I get the idea."

He waded across the beach and perched regally on a rock amid the crashing waves that had once torn at his soul. Surveying his swirling, frothy domain with his knees tightly tucked against his chest, Joe nodded his head in time to the beat of the tides beneath him. After a moment he raised his head toward the horizon and found that the merpeople had left. Though he was alone in the mist, he never noticed it. For the first time this evening, Joe did not feel lonely. He had become the surf, and his thoughts soared like a gull skimming the surface into the glint of the unknown before him. He couldn't see the end, because the horizon disappeared into its nightly gray. This unknowingness excited him. Rising from the ragged rock, he made his way past the tidal ebbs and back to his shirt and shoes. He fitted his shirt loosely over his torso without fully buttoning it and climbed the sandy hill to his vehicle. As he pressed the remote key in his hand, he watched the lights of the vehicle answer his silent sleight of hand. Then he took one last breath of the gray, noisy darkness and slipped inside car as he noted the comfort of artificially lit hues.

There were many things that he could not control in life. Some things, like the rhythm of the surf, he enjoyed not controlling. However, he knew he could seduce Gabriella beyond her point of no return, if he decided to try. That's what scared him the most. He operated more as a feline than she.

Backing the car of the lot, he turned around and merged onto the black highway pavement. It had been awhile since he drove a car barefoot. In some states it was against the law. Tonight it didn't matter. For whatever reason, he sensed that no authority would confront him. Life dealt like that. The only rules worth knowing were those that would be enforced. Otherwise, an individual was left to find their own, which usually reflected what they found meaningful.

In the familiar driveway of his home, Joe shut off the engine and headed for the front door. Ignoring the flashing lights on his answering machine, he showered and went straight to bed. In the early light of a new day, he rose to call up Joan on the East Coast.

"I met your merpeople last night," he confessed after she greeted him.

"They aren't my people," Joan calmly asserted. "What did they have to tell you?"

"Well," Joe began with a sigh. "They encouraged me to get to the heart of the matter."

"I see." Saying no more, she allowed the silence to become uncomfortably pregnant.

Joe stammered in a manly, breathless voice, "They're beautiful."

"Yes, they are," Joan responded softly. "What else?"

"When reality surfaces, it runs deep," he thoughtfully said. "They reminded me of a childhood friend. Her parents were friends with my parents. We often vacationed in Maine together."

"I didn't realize that you were that acquainted with the east coast," Joan observed.

"That happened a long time ago," Joe admitted. "I had forgotten about it until now. My friend died in a plane crash last summer. The merpeople reminded me of her."

"The merpeople may be bringing you a message. Maybe your friend has something to tell you from behind the veil, the transparent cloth between life and death," Joan suggested.

"She's not the only one," Joe confessed.

"I know. Joe, you are like a conduit between heaven and earth. The women of your life are giving you information for your project. Viewing life as the opposite gender gives you space to arrive at conclusions you might otherwise overlook or take for granted. Your friend on the other side seems light, like an interdimensional spirit."

"Oh yes," he said. "Liz harbored a bright, joyful spirit. I wonder what she has to tell me."

"Most likely something of an inter-dimensional nature," Joan reflected. Then she abruptly changed the subject, "How about taking Gabriella to breakfast? You've been working too hard, taking things too serious. Liz and the merpeople are here to remind you how light and bouncy life can be, which is sorta the way Donna, Carrie, and I see you. You seem above it all. Life is more than just rolling with the punches. Unlike the three of us, you actually fight back or deal with things, as if you are making life your own."

"I'm ready for a change of pace," Joe said with a laugh at himself in the mirror. "Thanks."

Chapter Eleven

Sometimes you have to
Find a new skill set

Reference Tune: *Over My Head*
----The Fray

JOE AND JOAN ended their conversation, leaving their phrases hanging in the air between them from the east coast to west coast. Their mutual understanding never touched the earth, remaining suspended until the next call. With so much more to be said, they waited patiently for the next moment to reveal their unfinished thoughts. Slowly replacing the receiver on console, Joe lingered in the air with the previous exchange, refusing to drop down from the flight. In this suspended state, he glanced out the front window and noticed that Gabriella had rolled into the driveway. Noting the precise, curt stop of Gabriella's sleek silver vehicle, he felt blessed that he hadn't heard her arrival but had witnessed it instead.

You can't get out of this one, boy, Joe told himself as he rose from the table to meet her outside.

Gabriella swiftly emerged from her car before flashing her dark eyes at him. Tossing her long dark hair to the side, she stood erect on spike heels without the hint of a wobble. Instead, the shoes seemed to be extension of her legs, which dazzled Joe from under the hem of her short dress.

Drat, he thought. *She looks too good, and I'm too easy. Figure it out, Joe.*

Succumbing to the heat of the moment, Joe calmly approached her. Cupping his hands around her cheeks, he slowly kissed her until he detected a quiver in her legs that touched the earth beneath them. Then he wiped a tear that had fallen from Gabriella's eye and closed his eyes for a moment. He didn't want to see her hurt, though he stopped at apologies. Gabriella was in her world, and he in his. Wrapping his arms firmly around her, he brought her to the mists of the beach, as he lingered on the words aired to Joan. As if on cue, Gabriella remained silent, returning his kiss with deep succulent admissions. Joe gave up his resistance. His head still swirled with the moist winds of the beach ringing in his ears. Opening his eyes for a quick survey of his surroundings, Joe decided to steal this private moment and lifted the woman into his arms.

Watching her eyes close, he felt her swoon before hurrying over the threshold of the front door. Though he sensed a slight hesitation in Gabriella's shoulders, she did not protest. She smiled lightly with smug confidence in his ability to engineer his way past any obstacle in his own home. It became apparent to Joe that she had broken and entered his home with minimal effort. He admired her machinations. Closing the door behind him, he carried his prize to the couch. Though he knew that the win was illusive, he was proud that he had managed to carry this much off. Gabriella moaned lightly as he nuzzled her. Finding her unspoken words very reassuring, Joe pinned her down with the weight of his body, while taking care not to be too imposing.

"Joe," she whispered in his ear.

"I'm a man of few words," he cautioned, persisting with a series of light kisses. This admittance provided the best explanation that he could offer for his actions. Under the circumstances, he declined her request to talk. Joe absentmindedly offered, "I prefer equations and schematics."

Gabriella giggled slightly with a laugh that emanated from deep within her belly. Joe stopped and examined her. Suddenly she had become his Buddha. Aroused, he lowered his head and groped for the origin of such a hearty laugh. Dwelling inside her, he sought her beaconing light as he plunged into the waters of a misty depth and merged with the milky waves. Then he soared with her for a moment before bringing her into his own steely gray, where finally they connected. As he plunged beneath the surface of superficiality, suddenly nothing else mattered except the fact that he had her. Contented with each other, they ceased to swim in the distance between them before lapsing into the space of each other's arms. Together they drifted into a fathomless sleep, where their collected consciousness eroded eventually by high noon.

After having spent several hours underneath him, Gabriella gently pushed Joe to the side of the couch so that she could get up. Joe acknowledged her with a slight smile, rolling over into the empty space that she had left. Out of the corner of his eye, he watched her get dressed in the bright shadows. Neither of them spoke.

After tightly clasping the bra around her breasts with a smile, Gabriella quickly buttoned her shirt over the lacy garment. Then she brushed her hair back and stepped into her heels. She turned and faced Joe one more time before leaving.

"See you at work," she announced in a hushed voice.

Joe blinked and she disappeared out the door. His mind continued to savor their foggy encounter, and the release that he had experienced within its lost confines. He valued the times that they communicated in silence. Gabriella had taken the past away, melting it like an alchemist. The transformation of spirit proved incredible. Together they had forged a new beginning in the diminished light of a world gone away.

Chapter Twelve

Not every adventure
Is worth leaving home

Reference Tune: *Sloop John B.*
----The Beach Boys

JOE DECIDED TO take the rest of the day off and return to the beach later in the afternoon. He would catch up with Gabriella once they had time to process the experience. Now that he knew that he and Gabriella weren't going anywhere, he wanted to see whether the merpeople had gone. These inter-dimensional souls had inspired his recent efforts with Gabriella. Now that he had brought the relationship forward in time, he wanted reassurance. He felt vulnerable after his intimate encounter with Gabriella. Liz---and too many other people and events in his life---had seemingly passed away in an eye blink.

After parking the car at the top of the bluff, Joe skated down grains of sand to the place where he had spent the moonlight. Hints of foggy mist hung around the streaks of sun that struck the surf. A light sense of clarity prevailed in the salty air, with just enough haze to prevent inevitable conclusions, which sewed mystery back into the winds of life. Finding his rock, he stood on top of it and scanned the horizon. He smiled when he saw several merpeople bobbing up and down in the distance waves.

Realizing the nearby beachcombers were oblivious to their merpeople's presence, Joe squatted on the barnacle-hewn rock and listened carefully. He appeared to be the only one on the beach aware of this other dimension. Awed by the duality of this experience, Joe quieted as his mind danced with the lighthearted spirits in the golden-flecked waves.

"We're pleased that you made up with Gabriella," several of the merpeople told him.

Joe took a deep breath and rolled his eyes slightly, unaccustomed to people that were half-fish stepping into his love life. Then he squinted past them into the stillness of the line of the horizon.

"Can we change the subject?" he insisted. "I don't see what Gabriella has to do with this."

Not replying, the merpeople floated softly in the waves. Regardless of whether they had an answer, they knew better than to continue the subject and respond to his direct question. They didn't want Joe to run from them.

Satisfied they wouldn't torment him, Joe relaxed and leaned back on the rock. His countenance brightened, expressing relief and joy that he had their attention. Dropping his bare feet down in the swirling currents of the waters, he tested the aqueous vibe for emotional currents. He had lost a friend in a plane crash. She no longer existed on the physical plane. Presently he possessed low tolerance for insensitivity on a matter that remained close to his heart. This pain threshold had nothing to do with his relationship with Gabriella. It seemed obvious to Joe that his affair with Gabriella had happened despite the perpetually tenacious state of the feelings that gripped him. The problem with maturity was that his relationship with the feeling world had become more refined, like the high vibrations of a violin. Somehow these vibratory frequencies had never left him. Instead, they resounded fully between his two ears, providing his life with an ongoing symphony. With maturity, he had learned the beat of his own life in relationship with the great OM of the universe, Joe found that an un-orchestrated life seemed worthless. Where came the music when you needed it the most? He quickly dropped events and circumstances that didn't follow the elegant beat. Anything that twanged with the strings of his heart would simply not be heard.

When he looked up from his feet, he saw his friend, Liz appearing in the steamy vapor over the shaded portion of the waves. Surprised, he consulted the merpeople sunning in the ocean. They only seemed more animated over the encounter.

"Interdimensional beings are so much more fun and trustworthy than spirits working through karma," the merpeople reassured him.

Joe blinked and rose to his feet. The shock of the cold water on his legs assured him that he wasn't hallucinating. Liz smiled and excitedly ran through the waves with a childlike skip. When she splashed some water drops in his direction, Joe laughed in spite of himself. Her playful spirit had not died.

I've missed you, he communicated without words.

Liz didn't say a word. Instead she kicked some more water in the air, making sure that Joe caught more of the spray. Almost drenched as the result of her endeavors, Joe responded with a few kicks of his own.

"What do you want to tell me?" he questioned the apparition. He knew better than to waste his time with spirits. Getting down to business, he confronted her, "Let me guess...You found the lost city of Atlantis during your scuba expeditions in the Mediterranean. That's why they sabotaged your family plane. That's why you quit speaking to me. You wanted to keep your findings all to yourself."

Liz grinned wryly. She mischievously shot a glance at him out of the corner of her eye. Still refusing to speak, she continued to splash him and shook her head in response.

So I am close to the truth, he replied nonverbally, crossing his arms over his chest and studying her further. "They killed you because you trespassed in the Pentarch's underwater city. You hoarded the information, thinking you and I weren't on the same wavelength. But, you were wrong. you know, I could have helped you with the information that I had. We could have shared notes, perhaps even have saved your life."

Intent on his dialogue with Liz, Joe never saw the huge wave coming that almost struck him down. Liz joyfully danced around him and rubbed her hands in glee. Thoroughly drenched, Joe searched the merpeople for support.

"Bull's-eye!" The merpeople waved at him. "You figured her out."

"Boy, did I ever," Joe said with a laugh as he wrung the water from his shirt.

Without another glance at Liz, he turned on his heels to go dry out on the beach. Sitting in the sand a safe distance from any encroaching tides, he peered again at the distant horizon. Liz had helped him remember how to play. Meanwhile, the merpeople had disappeared beneath the surface. They wanted to leave the friends alone in private.

Liz came and joined Joe. Sitting beside him, she began to relate her findings. Without facing her, Joe cocked his left ear toward her, paying close attention. Satisfied that she had conveyed the necessarily information, Liz promised to come visit him at his home to fill him in on other details. Joe's head throbbed with the implications of her story. Under the circumstances, his attention span fell short of their conversation. Hurriedly, he rose and climbed the sandy hill to the car. As he carried his soaked belongings under his arm, he intently concentrated on placing one foot in front of the other with a steady gait. He could feel Liz fade around him and let her go. A hot tear escaped his eye. As he wiped his face with the sleeve of his salty, wet shirt, he grieved her demise while trying to move forward with greater purpose in the resumption of their friendship. After reaching the top where he had parked his vehicle, he turned around and glanced at the beach below. Satisfied that Liz had left the scene, he noted the continued absence of the merpeople. The place had returned to its usual four-dimensional appearance. This obliging rearrangement soothed him.

"We still get along," he gratefully acknowledged, appreciating the fact that Liz and the merpeople had left him alone in his warmer, familiar, comforting world. Joe gave the misty air one last sniff before entering his car. The women in his life moved him to places almost beyond his comprehension. Here he stood, in the middle of it all with his two-way tapping endeavors and engineering innovations.

Upon returning to his home, he took a quick shower before calling Carrie. Joe knew Carrie also cultivated a secure inner sanctuary away from those intent on frivolity. Unlike others involved in his life, he felt safe exploring different worlds with Carrie and her companions, Joan and Donna. They had taught him love, whereas Liz appeared as a work in process. Gabriella represented a new beginning.

"I have friend on the other side who also tangled with the Pentarch's underwater structure," he told Carrie. "Only Liz wasn't as fortunate as Yanni. The Pentarch didn't realize that Liz had found Atlantis. The difference between this place and the one that you described in Maine is that there seems to be a Lemurian connection."

"You're right," Carrie affirmed, tracking Joe's information remotely. "Liz found another section of sunken Atlantis. This piece of Atlantis docked with Lemuria during the Great Cataclysm. I can visualize Blue Luminaries in the region."

"Yes, Liz did mention the hues of blue in the underwater cave," Joe recalled. "It seems that the Blue Luminaries are survivors from the Great Cataclysm."

Chapter Thirteen

Memories of loved ones

Roll in with the seasons

Reference Tune: *The Boys Of Summer*

----Don Henley

"HMM, IT APPEARS that the blue light connects to the spirit of the planet," Carrie observed. "It's has regenerative properties."

"We could all use some rejuvenation in this day and age," Joe said. "Although, Liz never mentioned it, I detect three portals associated with this particular portion of Atlantis-Lemuria."

"There are two in England," Carrie added. "One is at Chalice Well, and another site is located at Tintagel near Merlin's cave. The third portal can be found in a valley in Wales. It is in a sacred grove that appears almost ominous. The place scares away those who fear spirituality."

"The Druids descended from Lemurians. They partnered with the natives in northeastern Europe," Joe extrapolated. "The Druids must have continued using the portals over the centuries."

Carrie surmised, "Apparently, it's time for this uncovered piece of Earth's history to move forward."

Later in the afternoon, Joe received a call from Donna. Eagerly anticipating her revelations, he sat down in the most comfortable chair he could find, relaxing so that he could focus his attention on their conversation. Only the grip of his fingers on the receiver betrayed his intensity.

"Carrie and I worked it out," Donna began. "The Lemurian insurgents caused this portion of Atlantis to dock with this Lemurian land mass."

"How did they manage that?" Joe questioned.

"Apparently it was easy," Donna replied. "These Lemurians had prior knowledge of the Great Cataclysm, and sectioned off a portion of Atlantis for their escape. Using electronic techniques, they gridded the section to the previously sunken Lemurian continent. The Lemurian continent had a distinct composition as a result of the Serpentine attack. They used it against the Serpentines, who for some reason couldn't connect to their own devices."

"How?" Joe pondered out loud.

"Carrie might know," Donna said with a sigh, feeling slightly frustrated that they had hit another wall. "I planned to call her later tonight."

Donna and Joe hung up after agreeing to touch base early the next morning. Reclining in his chair after the phone call, Joe reflected silently on the possibility of a Lemurian underground during the time of Atlantis. Shaking his head over the thought of rebels riding a chunk of bedrock to a prescribed destination, one that had once been their home, he realized it had literally been an underground movement.

Feeling slightly dazed, Joe went to go lie down in bed. The butterscotch rays of the setting sun came through his window and brightened the room. Closing his eyes, he saw Liz enter his visualization. This time she metamorphosed into a tall, blond, blue-eyed Lemurian male. He realized that she had entered his past. In his dream the man handed him a small creature.

"Look," Liz the Lemurian told him. "The Serpentines altered the DNA of certain species. This is just a sample of their secret work."

"You've been around me for a long time," Joe remarked, focusing his attention on Liz's spirit rather than the strange creature. "I've seen this sample embedded in the rock history. It's a fossil now. Donna would know more about it. She's the geologist and has friends in paleontology."

Liz the blue-eyed Lemurian winked at him brightly. "Let Donna know that I sent you this. You were there when the inevitable Atlantean conclusion began. The story has to do with the information contained in the fossil."

Lost in this deep lucid sleep, Joe saw himself accept the live creature from the Lemurian's hand. Holding it close, he examined it further and found it had fossilized during the transfer from Liz's hands to his. Meanwhile, Liz's masculine counterpart faded into the golden haze of the western sun.

Joe blinked his eyes open in the pitch darkness of the room. Remnants of the dream swirled in his head as he peered into nothingness while regaining consciousness. Trying to reconnect the fragmented memory, Joe centered on the fossil. Then he made his way in the dark to his laptop down the hall. Joe did a quick search on the Internet, zeroing in on a picture of the fossil. He promptly e-mailed the description to Donna.

"I showed it to Carrie," Donna told him several hours later.

As promised, she called in the wee hours of the morning. Negotiating the three-hour time difference between them, Joe briefly dozed and awoke shortly before her call. This time he felt clearheaded, rather than lost in an endless dream state.

"What did Carrie say?" he asked curiously.

"We both agree that this creature became altered when everything was going hunky dory in Atlantis. We suspect that only the Lemurian insurgents knew what going on. These experiments were probably performed under the nose of the Atlanteans without being detected."

"I suppose that is one method of subterfuge. Make your move when it looks like everyone is getting along fabulously."

"We think that is what happened," Donna agreed. "This Orthoceras *fossil* stands out conspicuously in the rock record, encompassing the Ordovician to Triassic periods. It dates back 488 million to 199.6 million years ago. We can use this particular index species for gridding purposes now. Joan suggested using it as a homeopathic. There's certain amount of healing and protection that it offers us today, though, now that we understand the story, the sample appears almost hideous. I've never been so repulsed by a rock, ever."

Joe laughed softly, "You've been sensitized."

Donna chuckled and added, "It's a live rock."

"Only in the head of a geologist," Joe mused.

"Comes with the territory," she agreed. "We are in suspect terrain."

"We just didn't know it. I'm going into work early today. I need to catch up on some projects and check on Gabriella. I'll search for a schematic that mimics the repulsive frequency. Time to get back to work. Summer is gone."

Chapter Fourteen

Rough lives

Make the edges clearer

Reference Tune: *Wild, Wild West*

----The Escape Club

AFTER THE PHONE conversation with Donna, Joe gathered his bicycling gear and rode into work. As usual, the sleepy town didn't wake to his lively coming and goings. His habits didn't fit contrived rhythms, and Joe chose vacant side streets to avoid harassment. Often he caught the wistful eye of drivers daydreaming at traffic lights, while pedaling freely past traffic and down narrow, less frequented streets. Like the robins, he lived another life.

By seven, Joe arrived at the office building and turned the key in the door. He entered the office lab and encountered the individual who had purposely tracked his whereabouts this morning. Almost by instinct, she sat in front of the workstation where Dorothy often perched.

Without a word, Gabriella smiled when he affectionately gave her a soft peck on the cheek. Sighing languidly at him, she rose from the chair. He watched a light tremor run through her body and to the floor. Wide-eyed, Joe blinked several times at her so that he wouldn't melt. He noticed that she appeared rather proud of her effect on his countenance, though she didn't flaunt it. Instead she picked up her papers and headed for the exit. Then she paused for a moment and stood in the doorway. Tossing her long black hair to the side, she abruptly turned and faced him.

"José, you've been burning the candle at both ends," Gabriella said. Her lips grinned wryly as she flashed her dark eyes at him. "I always knew that you were a man with many lives. You're like a cat."

For a brief moment, Joe felt proud of himself for having elicited such a passionate response from Gabriella. Slowly regaining his senses, he retorted, "They have been tapping me for a long time. I just decided to take advantage of the situation. Besides, I enjoy winning. I don't want to be another victim. I have other partners in crime. Carrie, Donna, and Joan understand me. We have a lot in common." Without looking up, Joe unpacked his bags and pulled out some fresh clothes. "No time to talk. I need to shower and change my clothes."

"I know," Gabriella uttered slowly, stretching out her words as if she rolled Spanish "r"s at him. She intentionally kept her reply brief, so that it could be interpreted on many levels. For once she preferred remaining vaguely direct, which provided flexibility in her position, as well as Joe's life. Before leaving him for sunlit office down the hall, she told him, "Hurry back to work. I want in."

Joe chuckled to himself as he placed his gear at the desk. Then he hurried to the shower. Gabriella disappeared in the sanctuary of her office, while Joe returned to various projects in the lab without further interruption. Later in the afternoon, he walked outside the building to answer a phone call from Joan. He observed Gabriella watch him as he rushed out. Pacing back and forth across the small lawn, Joe spied her as she pretended that she had never seen him.

"Joe, we need to protect the Presidio with an Orthoceras. Then we'll grid it with the other missions," Joan suggested.

"Tell me about it," Joe encouraged her. "I feel nauseated just thinking about the place. It occurred to me this afternoon to focus on protecting the planet, given the history of the place. Occultists plan to counter Carrie's time wrinkle on Labor Day."

"I know. Carrie sensed it and e-mailed me. It's the same group that supports the cardinal. The cardinal is part of the Germain-Sauron duo from the *Lord of the Rings*. They persecute the MidEarth and those connected to it."

"Do you mean the group that violated her in childhood and in the hospitals?"

Joan sighed, amazed at how much Joe paid attention to the details of people's lives. "Yes, one and the same. However, we all need protection now, including those caught in their diabolic, human-trafficking exploits."

"You don't need to explain it to me," Joe said. "I know what you're talking about. My latest tap indicates that it runs even deeper, involving the Russian underground in an endgame. It is like another Armageddon."

"Remember, it's only a masquerade."

"That's what it so nauseating," Joe admitted. "It is all one big, deadly game."

"I understand," Joan said. "But, you're the one in the Wild, Wild West. Meanwhile, we'll run interference in the east."

"Thanks," Joe responded. "I think I'll bring Gabriella along. She's on to me."

"That's not such a bad thing," Joan surmised.

"If it gets any worse, I'll have to marry her," he confessed.

"It could be worse," Joan said with a laugh. "Just consider her a cohort. You'll get over it."

"Great idea, but I'm having too much fun now." Joe laughed heartily. "Talk you later. I'll let you know how it goes."

"What? Do you mean with Gabriella?" Joan teased slightly.

"No, the Presidio," he stated firmly.

Joe put his cell phone away and reentered the building. Waltzing into Gabriella's workspace, he proposed, "Want to help me find a fossil for the Presidio?"

"I'd thought you'd never ask," Gabriella said dryly. Fluttering her dark eyes, she quickly put her papers away and announced, "I've been waiting for this moment. I'll drive."

Joe smiled and left as Gabriella gathered her things. After joining him minutes later at the lab, she watched him shoulder his backpack. Together they hurried out of the office building, and walked to Gabriella's compact vehicle. Joe stowed his pack on the backseat before swiftly sliding on the passenger seat.

"Where's the fossil place?" Gabriella asked while starting the engine. Then she added without offering her hand, "I promise I won't offer any wise-guy comments. Deal? Shake on it."

"Deal," Joe said with relief, noting the absence of the handshake that would seal the deal. Leave it to Gabriella to keep him on his toes. Relaxing back in his seat, he provided directions to his favorite rock shop. Then he glanced at Gabriella with a tight smirk pulling at the corners of his lips, "We need an Orthoceras."

Gabriella humored him. "Of course."

Joe watched her back stiffen with resolve, despite her apparent lightheartedness. He contentedly leaned back even further, with his hands crossed behind him. He knew he had her.

"Yes, an Orthoceras," he confirmed. Then he added with a hint of omniscience, "Watch out for the *diablos*. There are a few cults at the Presidio along with the disposed Soviet leader and his green party. You know, the one that parties with the former governor, who married the human-trafficking section of the sabotaged Peace Corp, part of the coup d'état of 1963."

"What!" Gabriella exclaimed. Then, taking a deep breath, she resolutely eased her composure, "Okay, Joey. I got you. Now I know why you didn't like my story about the contaminated wine down the street. Say no more."

They spent only twenty minutes at Joe's favorite rock shop. Then they found the highway route to the Presidio and sped south. When they arrived at their destination, Gabriella parked on the street and they walked through the park. Joe hid the fossil in his right hand then searched for the best place to position it. Silently Gabriella gazed at him without being obvious and distanced herself from him a few feet. The thoughts swimming in her head minimized any conspicuous connection between the two. She wanted to observe him as well as the surroundings.

"Look, Joe," she nudged him as she abruptly stepped aside. For a moment, she resumed a more serious air then suddenly dropped it. "See those people parading around in black robes with horned figures on their back."

"Illumined *diablos*," Joe said.

"Oh," she answered as her eyes grew big and wide. Then she straightened, regaining her former sense of humor, "Where to now, Joey?"

"An investigator by the name of Mae Brussell researched the child abuse at the Presidio," Joe explained. "She discovered the link to the *diablos'* rituals, which involved the local military. Afterwards, she died from a sudden case of cancer as if she had been targeted with carcinogenic substances, sorta like the ones described by the girlfriend of the president's alleged assassin. They have some of Mae Brussell's research on file at a local university."

"Hey, how about planting the Orthoceras fossil under one of the trees near Fort Scott?" Gabriella suggested, ignoring the details that Joe provided. "Then let's get out of here until the place has a spiritual makeover."

"Great idea," Joe said with a nod. "The energy fits General Winfield Scott's mission concerning the Serpentines. I can slide it underneath a root system without moving any dirt."

Heeding her advice, Joe deposited the fossil appropriately, and the couple left the scene.

Once they were inside the vehicle, Gabriella immediately started the engine and asked, "Where to next, Joe?"

This time Joe noticed that she had not addressed him as Joey. Her manner had become more businesslike, reflecting the gravity of the previous undertaking. Though he never minded her playful ways, he realized that she now made it a point to be serious. Like watching a cat beginning to swish its tail in warning, Joe resolved to avoid alarming her further. He offered, "How about a bite to eat at Fisherman's Wharf?"

"Sounds wonderful, Joseph O'Connor!" she happily acknowledged, expressing sincere relief that Joe would no longer pressure her.

Joe smiled at the sound of his formal name. Following her suit, he remained in a heightened state of alert consciousness. The enchanted evening symbolized a new beginning. A romantic dinner for two soothed their traumatized souls after the reality check at the Presidio. Later that night, after dinner, Gabriella offered to drive him home, so that he would not have to ride his bicycle in the dark from the office.

"Would you like to share the evening with me?" Joe asked, kissing her goodnight with a subtle hint of sensuality. He wanted to seize the moment, preferring to avoid being alone tonight.

He watched her black eyes grow big again. Immediately Gabriella responded, "Now you're talking, Joe."

Chapter Fifteen

Regret is a senseless killer

Never live with it

Creates unbearable suffering in the living

And must be avoided at most costs

Reference Tune: *What Hurts The Most*

----Rascal Flatts

THE COUPLE LINGERED in each other's arms as morning sunlight streamed in the hallway outside the bedroom door. A soft ring emerged from the workstation near the kitchen. Hurrying to answer an important phone call, Joe streaked across the room to answer it without searching for his clothes.

Gabriella gazed at his unabashed performance while he exited. Then she tested him with a comment, "Please hurry. It must be the divine feminine."

Joe's hand appeared briefly at the doorway. Decidedly, he waved her away and out of his affairs. Satisfied with his singlehanded response, Gabriella quieted and put on Joe's dress shirt. Like a slinky feline, she followed him into the kitchen and found him seated at his workstation.

"Nice dress," Joe breathlessly told her, turning toward her. With a second's hesitation, he offered her a profile view after hanging up the phone. He rose from his chair to greet her.

The passion of the previous night clouded his thinking. Joe forgot himself, stepping into his natural attire without any reservation. Gabriella cautiously approached him so that she didn't disrupt his lack of self-consciousness. She treasured these moments when he occasionally lapsed into this stance, like a peacock displaying his full set of colors. As she drew nearer, she could tell that something far more serious had seized his thoughts. Suddenly Joe drew away, turning his back to her as he resumed his seat in front of the computer screen. Deciding to meet him halfway in his dazed state, Gabriella unbuttoned the shirt so that it would slide off her body and land on the floor. Leaning over his shoulder with the fullness of her breast touching the nape of neck, she gasped slightly when he allowed her to read an e-mail that he was typing.

Joe shuddered slightly, sensing her response. He persisted in silence. Joan had asked for more information on a mass shooting in Colorado. A gunman had showed up at a movie about a caped crusader. His jest left many people dead or injured.

Gabriella deftly pulled up a chair next to Joe and watched him check his two-way tap. Then he resumed typing. Joe glanced at her briefly, letting her know how much he appreciated her. His hand softly reached for her upper thigh, patting her there for an eternal moment. Then his hand fell away as he processed the information of the e-mail.

It's a decoy. Like the Colorado Springs fire, it is a ruse to get people away from the Colorado Rockies. But, there is more---a bigger scene elsewhere. The Trident missile base that was infiltrated when Gorbachev led the Soviet Union has been on high alert for the past month. They want to create an incident to embarrass the US president before the election. Like the aftermath of 9/11, the incident will serve to restrict the constitution even further, creating a state of martial law.

Gabriella rose and stood beside him. Kissing him softly on the cheek. She told him, "I'll leave you to your work, Joe. Send me a copy of the e-mail."

Joe looked up, reaching for her. Caressing her with his eyes, he nodded a gentle thanks. Gabriella grabbed his wrist firmly for a few seconds then let go and headed back to the bedroom. After a quick shower, she dressed before returning to the kitchen.

Tossing a pair of shorts in his lap, she told him, "Don't forget these. Even Superman wears tights."

Joe looked up at her, accepting the cup of green tea she handed him. She bent her head and kissed him again on the cheek. Leaning over his shoulder, she studied the last few lines of the e-mail he had written.

Go through the Baby Doe Mine and the Independence Mine to access the neuroscience mind-control lab and the missiles stolen during the Oklahoma City bombing. The government will want these finds, while parents will want their missing children back. You'll find homeless youth in the various caverns. Also, check out the cult north of San Antonio, and examine the local limestone catacombs for more lost children. The military-industrial complex has been programming these youngsters for years. The results of their experiments go mainstream---in advertising, films, books, Internet and social media. A researcher once referred to the process as "Killing Us Softly."

Joe stopped to put his shorts on. Then he stood up and took a few sips of his tea before warmly hugging Gabriella goodbye. "It is a ghastly event they've concocted with the movie about a caped crusader," he told her. "They're playing with the public's perception of reality, a deadly mind game. I wasn't planning to see it myself."

"Don't look at me," Gabriella said, winking at him before heading out the front door. She wanted to keep their encounter light. "My life is too action-packed for the movies. See you at work sometime, Joey."

He grinned and cocked his head to the side as he heard her words. Listening to the sound of her car backing out of the driveway, he returned to his work. After he completed his e-mail, he sent it to Joan, who would forward it to Larry and Eli. Joan had friends in high places, people who could follow through on the mission.

Joe grabbed a light breakfast and went to rest on the sofa, where he lapsed into a heavy sleep. Several hours later, he rose and rechecked his e-mail, noticing a response from Joan. She wrote that presidential-intelligence teams had located the Blues' base under the Rockies and that authorities had seized some advanced technology there. The find provided the silver lining to this terrible shooting. Joan wrote:

The caped crusader movie targeted a young reporter for hockey. She had witnessed a shooting at a Toronto mall and asked too many questions. Her investigation led to the same rival bootleggers who played a major role in the president's assassination concerning the TFX---the missile connection revisited. They also found the sporting goods company that made the carcinogenic clothing, detected by Carrie earlier. Stick to old sports gear for the next few years, until the radioactive material decays.

Joe finished reading the e-mail. Rubbing his hands over his forehead, he decided to give Gabriella a quick call. He knew that she would be at work by now, after a change of clothes at her place. Most likely, he thought, the next step would be to have her keep her clothes in one of his closets at home.

"What's up?" Gabriella asked him.

"I won't be in," he admitted. "I'm going to the beach after I finish here. There are a few things that I need to check on."

"Keep in contact," she insisted.

Chapter Sixteen

You either sell joy and love

Or make joy & love

Sell or make

Like death and life

Becomes a choice

Reference Tune: *Levon*

----Elton John

JOE DROVE TO his familiar beach, and left his car parked at the bluff. At high tide, the water covered the rock where he had sat during the previous night. This time he didn't walk all the way down to the surf. Instead he found a comfortable space midway, behind some tall grass. Though the water appeared calm, the reeds betrayed the wind as it intently airbrushed the shoreline. The merpeople swayed on top of the waves in the distance, seeming to be more in the sky than in the water. They seemed to be enjoying themselves. The merpeople didn't stop to acknowledge Joe's presence, though he felt they sensed his arrival. A silent song rose from the bouncy merpeople, and flew with the wind to the top of the cliff over his head.

The song carried a particular frequency to his ears, and he sat down to decipher its meaning. As he gazed into the blue atmosphere, he saw a disc-shaped spacecraft hovering above. An unmarked, gray airplane flew near the spaceship. The sight of the advanced technology enabled Joe to hear the lyrics of the quiet song.

It's powered by fusion.
The spaceship is so elegant.
What an exciting future awaits us in twenty years!

Joe stood to get a better view. Then he walked laterally across the bluff without descending any further towards the water. The spacecraft disappeared behind a cloud. The sight of the fusion-powered flying vehicle did not surprise him. He knew several scientists who had been killed for mentioning they had discovered fusion. Joe suspected that fusion was as old as the sun, and had existed on the planet for a long time. It was just a matter of harnessing the knowledge that had already been invented by spirit itself, sort of like catching a photon. Everyone caught photons; they just didn't know it. Nikola Tesla, the scientist behind the Philadelphia Experiment, had destroyed many men with his time travel experiments and almost killed himself at least once. He had devised a machine that could produce resonant frequencies that shook the Earth forcefully enough to produce an earthquake. He had built power towers in attempt to zap electromagnetic energies across the globe. His experiments were dangerous.

Tesla had no finesse, according to the books Joe had read. Tesla had worked in suspect terrain, including Colorado Springs and Manhattan. These were places were his inventions had literally gone to the dogs---or as Donna would say, "dogs-of-war"---and these dogs killed for sport. Though Tesla's society considered him poor and broken, rumors had it that the shadow government had stolen his notes by the time of his funeral. One might think that he would have learned, but Tesla didn't seem to care, preferring to blame others for his apparent lapses in social consciousness.

Tesla inspired the Manhattan Project, funded by robber barons intent on producing the nuclear bomb. World War II served as their testing lab for the ensuing nightmare. Those who had worked on the Manhattan Project, such as engineers in the heating/cooling industry, went into fossil fuels. Later, during the McCarthy era, they shifted into alternative-energy technology, which served as just another tool to market Tesla's fallen inventions. Tesla also had experimented with diathermy as well as cooling systems. The shadow military developed Tesla's weather-changing devices such as the High Frequency Active Auroral Research Program (HARRP), while industry employed Tesla's designs in manufacturing heating and air conditioning units. Consequently, a complex---rather than a marriage---was born, courtesy of the military-industry relationship. Authorities dubbed the relationship the military-industrial complex, which reflected a much deeper psychological hang-up than many would admit, though it constituted a codependency of which the creators seemed shamelessly proud. The creators birthed a new racket.

The same underground bootleggers harassing the WWI pacifists supplied the top military officers with boozed during World War II. Prohibition never ended until Hitler's new order, the Third Reich, came into existence. By the twentieth century, the establishment had learned that alcohol and ethanol ran wars. Research carried out at the Tavistock Institute had given the perpetrators harmful knowledge regarding what it took to break the human mind. During the Vietnam War, the self-medication of choice had become cannabis, and business in the Golden Triangle thrived. They had stolen Tesla's technology to create mind-altering frequencies from which there seemed no way out.

Carrie simultaneously had wrinkled time and withstood a spiritual attack. She accomplished this though the use of subtle energies, in contrast to the dramatic voltages produce by Tesla's currents and power towers. Her approach was much safer, which Joe appreciated. He knew that three amps were enough to kill a person. Thirty milliamps were enough for low-grade, neural paralysis. Though the phrase represented an oversimplification, the advice in electronics resounded: "It's the amps that kill you,"---rather than the voltage amount. By comparison, it took one hundred thousand to one and a half million volts to produce a nonlethal stun gun.

The trick in moving intact from one inertial frame to another involved the creation of what Tesla termed a 'doorway.' He jolted his subjects from one timeframe to the next, whereas Carrie chose a more holistic approach, accounting for cellular biology and molecules of emotion. Passages between two frames of references could be made simply by changing the electromagnetic frequencies. In preference to her particular time wrinkle, the vibrational frequencies were generated by desire and emotion. The desire to transcend or go beyond certain circumstance altered her physiology, because it created a space for more light to enter. Human emotions such as love and grief overwhelmed the oscillating system until surpassing the threshold energy state. The overall result provided a quantum leap into a different future. Emotions could be fueled like fusion due to the involvement of the limbic portion of the brain, which motivated soul travel. In this manner, surviving sailors from the Philadelphia Experiment were carrying the souls of those missing on the physical plane across the time dimension to a safe place known as the future. The human body operated as a semiconductor, entertaining currents less than half a milliamp. Most *chi gung* practitioners and transcutaneous electrical nerve stimulation (TENS) devices generated currents of 5 milliamps or microamps for healing purposes.

If they threw this sort of energy into the Schumann waveguide, the eight-Hz frequency layer that encircled the globe, they could resonate this energy with anyone tapping into an alpha state. The problem was that the Serpentines had used Tesla's power towers to tap into this eight-Hz layer. Considering the complexities, Joe's gaze turned from the floating merpeople to the ocean surrounding them. During the American Revolution, a church called Trinity Wall Street had sided with the British. Later church attendees, calling themselves Federalists, established a mission house. Missionaries served in various trade routes established by the British Empire under the East India Trading Company. Trinity Wall Street became Alexander Hamilton's place of worship, and he had run the new US government's money as treasurer. In addition, he even operated his own bank with General McDougall of the American Revolution. Originally called the Bank of New York, it still existed today as Bank of New York Mellon. All these people and their associations had known about the time wrinkle in India during the 1700's. They tied the bank into the financial guru who operated the spice trade and pulled the puppet strings for the East India Trading Company.

Joe took a whiff of the salty air as he studied the carefree flight of gulls that dove beneath the surface of the water. He detected an energetic trine connecting Trinity Wall Street with the towers at University of Dallas and Trinity University. Good or bad, trines and triangles created power vortexes. Some provided stability, such as those found in Da Vinci's art, whereas those used in ancient Egypt could be used to bring in alien frequencies of a destructive nature. The two towers at these places of higher education shared energy with the twin towers of 9/11. This device made by Tesla created an energetic doorway that would alter time during the routine military exercise that preceded the network collapse. As with the aftermath of 9/11, the relationships sustaining these places of higher education were particularly oil-soaked. Such contrast with the fusion-powered spacecraft was profound. One vehicle soared elegantly, whereas the use of 9/11 as a vehicle appeared diabolical.

Joe continued walking across the bluff and away from the merpeople. Something else caught his attention south of the beach. As he moved closer to the vision, he recognized a familiar shape and light.

Chapter Seventeen

The Nevers in Life:
Never give out, never sell out, and never give in
Never sit out a dance
Unless you're tired

Reference Tune: *I Hope You Dance*
----Lee Ann Womack

THE APPARITION GUIDED Joe's steps, while remaining in view two meters ahead. The interdimensional woman led his way over the small, sandy dunes dotted with sprawling vegetation. With a light nod, Joe recognized the female spirit with the auburn hair and purple dress, the one who drifted into his dreams.

As he scanned the waterfront for other signs of humanity, the shoreline remained vacant, though there remained only a hint of autumn in the sea breeze. Air rose from the cool waters and interfered with the rays of the sun heating the tiny, silicated grains of sand. Fall announced itself with the transition of solar heating to passive cooling. Continuing to loom in the distance, the woman's form quivered like heat waves emanating from a hot surface. She didn't leave him alone on the beach. As she seemed to envelope herself in his thoughts, white ribbons of light shimmered around her contours to the sky above. Despite this subtle motion, she lingered in a self-sustained steady state. The transparent waves that surrounded her vibrated at a particular high frequency and radiated without a thermal gradient.

Most scientists classified the physical body as a semiconductor. Cellular components such as lipids acted as insulators, whereas minerals served as conductors. The hollowness of the DNA structure with its extended hydrogen atoms on the inside proved superconductive. Compared to a biological system, Tesla's technological derivatives in solar collection and energy transport didn't work as well. They only looked good on paper and in futuristic design, provided one had a taste for steely glass, dull metal, and high maintenance. These designers were beholden to the distributors of cold-pressed vegetable and animal matter, which took thousands of years. The proponents of fossil fuels also profited in human trafficking, and could not possibly appreciate free energy. A healthy human body possessed the innate ability to prevent death by fever or overheating of components. The Nazi corporation that sold aspirin could not be expected to rely on biology for homeostasis. Even Tesla understood the use of diathermy in immunity. Diathermy had been used more than a hundred years ago to successfully treat lung conditions with various frequencies of thermal radiation, which targeted specific tissues. Collateral research during this period found that disease could be annihilated through the application of specific frequencies without any side affects. One researcher measured the specific oscillating frequency of various microbes like virus and bacteria, but as with Tesla, his work had been secreted by competing interests in the military-industrial complex.

Tesla's inspiration came from extraterrestrials, the same ones advising MacArthur. These extraterrestrials represented celestial souls on the other side, who aided the spiritual battle on the planet. From his days spent as researcher in Atlantis prior the Serpentines' clandestine development of the

Orthoceras, Tesla's soul remembered the superior technology employed during that civilization. Though he managed to fuse a pure hybrid from celestial knowledge and Atlantean endeavor, the application of this technology to the human spectrum failed. In place since the assassination of Lincoln, the shadow government seized his papers and implemented faulty technology that didn't work. The human factor and the natural world remained absent in the design, which had evolved from a technically superior civilization, and had sunken on its own terms. Fortunately, Tesla managed to get his notes to US Presidents and the Kennedys before the shadow government slipped a lethal drug into a drink one night and ran off with his papers. They killed Tesla to silence his protests concerning the use of the atomic bomb. With him went the hope for a sensible end to WWII. After the war, the shadow government persecuted all nuclear protesters with a crucible built by a front man named McCarthy. Presently, Joe knew of a company foundation that busily implemented Tesla's information, and that company literally had missed the boat when it came to human factors.

The recovery of the sailors missing from the three Philadelphia Experiments required another lifetime, something that eluded Tesla technology. Some souls missing since the time wrinkle of the 1700s were rescued along with those of the Philadelphia Experiment. Questions arose concerning the details of the pre-American Revolution time wrinkle, one that had involved the East India Trading Company and Marco Polo's spice route. The inter-dimensional woman in front of Joe had been part of the recovery, though another generation had been required. The fragmented souls had to be brought back in harmony with the natural world, which meant cycles of life and death according to the human dimension. The missing sailors and gurus incarnated into another lifetime, supported by a network of love and desire. The rebirth involved icons from the multidimensional world as represented by the woman on the beach today. She opened the door to former planetary inhabitants of fairies, leprechauns, and elves, who constituted a spirited group. This multidimensional approach made the all the difference in the world between merely surviving and actually thriving. Bridging the imagination of the human spirit made life meaningful and worthwhile. The bridge restored life from the Grays to a multidimensional one complete with the colors of the rainbow, not just black and white or various shades of gray.

For these reasons, Joe never implemented Tesla technology. Though some remained reliably in the Light, celestials could flip one way or another---go dark and become calcified gods who demanded worship and human sacrifice. As in ancient Greece, the insensitive intervention in planetary affairs often proved detrimental to human affairs. Their grandiose schemes and manipulations isolated them from the dance of life itself. Like wallflowers at a celebration, they preferred to sit out any heartfelt interaction. Though Tesla's work could be considered brilliant, it also served as a loaded Faustian contract that lethally scorched the high-flying sons of Daedalus. Those who didn't listen to the fallen angels suffered in the Philadelphia Experiment, but they kept their souls in the long run. The same could not be said for Tesla, who allowed his technology to be misused and lost in the end.

The inter-dimensional woman on the beachhead directed Joe to a patch of red clover that grew on the bluff. Smiling, Joe bent over the groundcover to scan for a stem with four leaves. Four-leaf clovers pointed to the time dimension and were considered lucky. An individual was lucky if he or she didn't need to rely on the time dimension. Saint Patrick had used the symbology to distinguish the Serpentine Vatican from the Christian Church.

Those who sought to kill the spirit of the planet would not honor the triad of father, son, and spirit, which amounted to two generations and an essence. Rebirth and spirit did not fit their vampirish agenda. By the time of the American Revolution, a hearty attempt by the human race for spiritual freedom from the serfdom of the Roman Empire corporate oligarchy took shape. The Grays and Serpentines countered with own trinity, which spiritualized corporate generations and made a new religion. The conglomerate spirit became the third entity of their trinity. Corporations could legally live on forever and with protection. Like money, the energy of a triangular vortex could be good or bad; the components of a trinity included a parent, progeny, and spirit. When the planning of 9/11 occurred in the 1980's, Trinity Wall Street was gridded with two particular towers from private universities in Texas. Funding remained the same. The occultism partially contributed energetically to the collapse of the twin towers in New York, which also had a base with a Russian occult group. The Russian cult conducted ritual imagery of collapsing towers, which represented masculine power. This negativity was coordinated with in-house occultism on US soil, which had been fused with the crucible lit during the McCarthy hearings of the 1950s. As he scoured the clover patch, Joe finally realized that these were the same groups that had energetically interfered with Carrie's time wrinkle.

Joe looked up at the inter-dimensional woman near the clover patch to let her know that he wasn't having any success at finding a four-leaf clover. Under the circumstances, this issue had started to concern him. An inverse for the trinity counter grid was needed. He didn't know where to begin, and suddenly he wasn't feeling so lucky. While some World War II sailors had been sent to the Pacific front for execution, others continued the business of the East India Trading Company and flew contraband for Chiang Kai-Shek.

This next chapter in China's opium wars became another exercise in Hegelian dialectic. Both communists and nationalists were sponsored by corporate oligarch interests and played against each other. This codependency dynamic had been set up in the preceding century.

The multidimensional woman smiled warmly at him. Then she whispered in the wind. Joe paused and watched the ruffled patterns of bowing stems and tall grasses in the turbulence.

You must bring nature back in. After you do the inverse, elevate the grid with nature.

Chapter Eighteen

Love accommodates the tides of passion

Reference Tune: *Any Way You Want It*

----Journey

JOE STOPPED LOOKING for a four-leaf clover in the patch, and followed the inter-dimensional woman to a small cove. While he waded in the water, Joe watched her disappear in the foamy waves as the wind picked up momentum. The wind brushed through his dark hair, and he turned his focus inward for a moment. Scooping up some salty water in his hands, he splashed his forehead lightly and gazed at the sunset.

Blinded by the light, Joe shaded his vision for a clearer view. Solutions to problems raced through his head as his thoughts centered on the next tasks. He could counter-grid the perverse trinity arrangement with auditory tapes on developing a prosperity consciousness. Joan could place the taped recordings on advanced manifestation in her portal with the light energy circle. This arrangement countered any fear-based financial structure threatening to collapse a system rooted in ancient Londinium, a former Serpentine fort during the Roman Empire. This task completed the inverse.

Special interests strangled any natural capitalistic intention since the time of the American Revolution. The concept of natural capitalism spiritualized money in a manner that harmonized with the planet. Perhaps this symbolized the significance of the four-leaf clover in luck. Like the natural world, the growth of money took time. A person became lucky if they managed time. Part of wealth involved minimizing one's carbon footprint. Many of his rich friends wore T-shirts with holes, shopped at thrift stores, didn't mow their lawns, and exchanged poems instead of gifts.

Searching for deeper explanations, Joe's focus centered on the Pebble Mine in Alaska and the mines in South Dakota. A call from Donna interrupted his thoughts, though he sensed that she was the perfect person for further discussion concerning the hazards of open-pit mining. He pulled his cell phone from his back pocket, and moved away from the ocean's spray.

"It is more than just the physical environment," Donna told Joe when he explained his latest sojourn. "It is a spiritual assault on the Earth that dates back to the Serpentine-driven Inquisition of the Dark Ages."

"Keep going," Joe said.

"Ownerships of the mines can be traced to a network of corporations related to Freeport Copper, a sibling of the Freeport Sulphur Company. Researchers such as Lisa Pease and Jim DiEugenio linked Freeport Sulphur to the JFK assassination. They found that the subsequent character assassination served as a coverup for the president's murder by those who were into such things," Donna explained, after taking a deep breath. Noting Joe's silence, Donna continued, "The individual who runs Freeport Copper also operates another university associated with the perverse trinity grid. This college employed Tesla's technology in the design of its chapel for energetic enhancement. Its academic connections include the Ohio government in the 2004 election recount, Disney and Raytheon's participation in 9/11, the New Orleans underground, and mind-control investigators of the 1960's like Eli Lilly."

"Sounds like Captain Hook and his pirate ship," Joe remarked.

"That's the issue," Donna admitted. "The turret architecture and its name is a direct reference to the pirates of the Asian spice trade. Even though they disguised themselves as Jesuit missionaries associated with the East India Trading Company, they fooled no one."

"They ran with the Boston Brahmins," Joe speculated.

"Yes, unholy Roman Serpentines and Protestant missionaries working together for power and greed," Donna concluded. "Xavier represented Ignatius, who worked for one of the Spanish kings during the Inquisition. This king infringed on the preexisting spice trade operated by the wandering progeny of Abraham. The Roman Empire consisted of severed fragments of Roman legions left to fend for themselves after Constantine moved out of Western Europe."

"I think there's more. The Serpentines have been persecuting souls as far back in history as the destruction of Planet Mu."

Donna paused to track the timeline, "Yes, I think you're right. Spiritual persecution underlies the story of the Lost Boys from the *Peter Pan* epic. The souls surfaced as the Blue Luminaries described by Carrie. Remember, she visualized Blue Luminaries at the underwater cave that Liz found. The bedrock was formed from the docking of sinking Atlantis with a previously sunken portion of Lemuria."

"Now it is easier to understand how the Lemurian insurgents countered a Serpentine problem with the homeopathic remnants of a Serpentine attack," Joe observed. "The homeopathic remedy was literally carved-in-stone. The remedy matched the vibrational frequency of the disguised Serpentine genetic experiments during Atlantis. The combination produced a quantum effect that they used to escape, physically airlifting their embedded underground network to safety, while still keeping it underground. It is an amazing metaphorical feat of engineering."

Donna paused, swallowing hard before resuming, "I need to discuss the destruction of Planet Mu with Carrie. She'll be able to pick up on the Lost Boys, and how they became Blue Luminaries in the Pentarch's underwater park."

Joe ended the call with Donna, and waited for a ring from Carrie. Fifteen minutes passed between phone calls, giving him some time to reflect. He barely heard the sound of the ringtone over the thunderous ocean tide.

"Hello," Joe began. Finding another rock closer to the water's edge, he sat down. His extended time at the beach was turning into social occasions. Much of the information gleaned from these conversations would be transformed into electronic components for his project, the job that would probably earn hundreds of millions for his company. Hanging out the ocean shore with a cell phone glued to his ear was a worthwhile endeavor, though the approach was unusual.

"Donna called and asked me to check on the Lost Boys from the destruction of Planet Mu," Carrie stated when she heard Joe answer. "The Serpentines killed their children's parents on the home planet. Several hundred male children became stuck in the soul transport between Mu and Lemuria. For some reason, the female children never survived the soul transition to the Lemurian continent. Unfortunately, the children could not incarnate, because the parents had died. They remained suspended in another dimension. Meanwhile, the Serpentines continued their genetic experiments in Atlantis, and transformed earth spirits---for example, the elves into gnomes and dwarves, and the water spirits into merpeople. One Serpentine scientist managed to infiltrate the realm of the Gauds, but they caught him just as he made off with a hair sample from the goat god known as Pan. The Serpentines managed to seed the DNA sample with an entrapped elf named Peter, who was rescued by a green fairy. Peter mated with a Green fairy, the second cousin to a Blue fairy named Tinkerbell. They birthed their progeny inside the petals of a water lily, where the cross-pollination had taken place. Although the infant started out very tiny, the genetic anomaly grew to the size of a small boy with both fairylike and elflike qualities, except he possessed the spirit of the perpetually immature, fun-loving goat Gaud. The earth spirits called him Peter Pan. Because Serpentines often kill the results of their experiments as a way of destroying the evidence against them, Peter Pan ran from the very beginning. Though his three parents were killed by the Serpentine purge, Peter and Tinkerbell managed to find their way to Neverland. The trauma of the loss lured them to the same dimension as the Lost Boys, who had attracted them with their blue luminescence like a lighthouse. Being fully grown, the Lost Boys adopted Peter as their older brother, after he figured out how to materialize in their dimension."

"Hmm, sounds familiar," Joe commented. "I've never heard this story in the multidimensional tradition."

"Oh there's more," Carrie insisted. "The Lemurian insurgent, who set the Great Cataclysm in motion, befriended Peter. Peter served as his window to the Serpentine experimentation, which inspired the destruction of the Serpentines' crystal. Peter nicknamed the insurgent Windy, because he thought that the fellow was just telling him fairytales. Nobody in Atlantis took Windy seriously, which served as his comic cover. The result became the cosmic mistake of the century. Windy always joked and did comedy routines with his girlfriend. When Windy the storyteller died creating the

Great Cataclysm and inadvertently freed the souls of the Lost Boys, Peter decided to pay closer attention to Windy's stories posthumously."

"Well, it's never too late for a good story," Joe responded.

"Never. As a result, the Lost Boys, Peter, and Tinkerbell decided to stay in Neverland, occasionally appearing out of dimension to deal with Captain Hook throughout the ages."

Chapter Nineteen

Don't waste time

Questioning the emotions of love

Spend time between the satin sheets instead

Reference Tune: *Call Me*

----Blondie

"LET ME GUESS," Joe began, "The Captain Hook of today persists in annihilating the spirits of the planet through dummy corporations that poison it and human DNA."

"Great start," Carrie resonated. "He also drilled into the MidEarth."

"And the Gulf oil spill?" Joe questioned.

"Yes, it served as a cover for more tapping into the earth's spirit," she informed him. Then Carrie toyed with a phrase, "Earth spirits are us. I'm sensitive to taps in that realm. Ultimate control of the project remained in the hands of the Serpentines that Hook serves, so the tap eventually transforms into a resource drain if not stopped in time."

"Keep going," Joe responded, but then a doubt crossed his mind. "How does Hook get away with all the poisoning?"

"Through the calculated placement of government-sponsored officials and connections derived from the old East India conglomerate," Carrie expounded. "That's how Hook snatched the money strings of all the major banks in the United States. Remember, the Serpentines took over the government after the assassination of Lincoln. Ever since, the battle cry for the nation has been 'Industry, industry,' which was managed by the military establishment that seized the government."

"Oh," Joe sighed, regaining his composure after almost falling off his rock. He decided to stand and stretch. Then he wandered closer to the surf, letting the moist foam rush over his toes, while being careful not drop his cell phone in the wet sand. Next time, he promised himself, he would bring a waterproof cover with him to the beach, or design one to bring.

"Larry and Donna told me that the oil spill contributed to the activation of a major fault," Carrie persisted, ignoring Joe's sigh. "The fault line runs from New Orleans to Chicago and is geologically related to the present seismic activity along the Continental Divide. Local aerospace industries are using Tesla's technology to promote an earthquake in the region."

"The line of the artificial fault delineates our real friends," Joe murmured dryly.

"Stay out of it," Carrie instructed. "Protect your own space."

"I know. The Serpentines and Grays wage earthquake and environmental hazard wars in the Midwest." After a brief pause, another thought formed in his mind, "Where does Hook fit into the cosmic scheme of things?"

"Joan figured that Hook came from Sirius and operates the Black Dog occult group. They serve as the torturers for the Serpentines."

"No surprise there," Joe replied as he turned from the beach and slowly climbed the sandy hill. "It's time for me to head back into the office. I have a few minor details to add to my latest project. I also need to update my earthquake preparedness kit."

"Great idea. You are in the middle of things, being in the Wild West," Carrie chimed in. "I gotta finish up here quickly. I'm meeting Donna and her husband Eli for dinner tonight."

"Say hi for me," Joe said, ending on a happy note. "Talk to ya later."

Joe left the beach and drove home. After a shower and an early dinner, he drove to work. As he parked his car in one of the stalls, he noticed that Gabriella and a few others were working late. He went inside the building and peered through the doorway of her office.

"Joan wants you to contact her at this number," Gabriella greeted, carefully avoided public displays of affection tonight.

Joe appeared perplexed. There had been no texts, e-mails, or voice messages from Joan on his various machines. He wondered why Joan had gone through Gabriella to reach him. Rechecking his cell phone, Joe noticed that no information had been recorded.

"Joan and Larry suspect that their lines at Woodsport are tapped, so Joan left an urgent message with the receptionist," Gabriella explained, rising from her desk and walking with him to his workstation down the hall. She pointed at the note left on Joe's desk. "I saw it on your desk when I checked on things here. There are no secrets around here. I know you, Joey."

Without a word, Joe ran his fingers through his hair and tried to fathom the meaning of the message. "Thanks for covering for me," he told her.

Satisfied, Gabriella turned to exit the room, leaving Joe alone to communicate with his various devices. Pausing for a moment to reflect on the change of circumstances, Joe watched her go and returned to his thoughts without saying anything further. At this point in life, he recognized that he didn't have an explanation, nor did he feel that he owed Gabriella one. She shot a glance at him, subtly out of the corner of her eye, before completely disappearing. He knew she enjoyed it when he appeared loss for words. Without bothering to waste any more time in analysis, Joe dialed Joan's number.

"Great. It's you," Joan answered excitedly. "I have caller ID now, so I can screen calls."

"My work lines are safe," Joe calmly assured her, getting straight to business. "We anticipate this sort of intrigue in the Valley. As you know, it's the Wild West. My company developed a device for calling in and out without being detected. Maybe we'll market it one day, but for now it gives us an edge in the business world, and we do mean business."

"I'd rather have them clean up the tappers," Joan said with a laugh. "It's like putting kids in plastic buckets instead of getting the drunks off the road. I can still remember the days when seat belts were optional."

"My entire company says they can remember the days when seat belts were not a requirement!" Joe retorted with a light chuckle. "That's why, the device isn't on the market yet. We haven't crossed that line into policing."

"Hook wants to crash healthcare and the banks," Joan revealed, returning to the focus of their conversation.

"I know," Joe said. "Donna, Carrie, and I talked about it today while I was at the beach."

"What are you getting on your two-way taps?"

"I don't know. I haven't been around to check them. I need to make a few adjustments to the projects after our ocean-view discussions. I was just getting to those alterations now."

"Here's another one," Joan cautioned him. "Hook and his conglomerates have been tracking Carrie since she was twenty years old. Larry and I figured this out earlier this morning."

"Does Carrie know?"

The implications slowly dawned on him. Something occurred during Carrie's extended hospital stays that warranted Hook's undivided attention. Joe wondered how a two-year-old could pose such a threat to a mighty world corporation held spellbound by a powerful villain.

"No," Joan told him. "I want a protective shield in place before sharing this information any further."

"Understood. Hook's people posses an understanding of past lives. They track the energy, using the advantage of prior knowledge to attack unsuspecting individuals. It's a nasty business, and a subtle form of mind control. Their victims never have much of a chance."

"Tell me about," Joan said with a sigh. "If this is true, we're all on the steep end of the spiritual growth curve."

"Knowledge isn't everything," Joe said. "Somehow Carrie eludes them, whether or not she knows it, though she must have be aware of the situation on the spiritual level. Otherwise she never would have made it this far."

"Tell me about it," Joan repeated with an air of resignation in her voice. "What do you suggest?"

"Hit him back," Joe simply insisted.

"Well, I suppose, though it seems counterintuitive. The concept arises from the more instinctual aspects of a human being."

"Just do it harder and more decisively," Joe countered.

"How?" she asked before instantly recalling her training in *chi gung*.

"An aikido move," Joe responded. "He can hit harder than us. Just send Hook back on his own reflection."

"Would an octagonal *feng shui* mirror in the portal work?"

"Mirrors and crucifixes work on vampires," Joe said. "So why not their minions?'

Chapter Twenty

Every now and then
You have to go for
Breaking that glass ceiling

Reference Tune: *Thunderstruck*

----Thunderstruck

LONG AFTER GABRIELLA and the others had departed, Joe finished his work in the office and arrived home late in the evening. Entering through the front door shortly before midnight, he grabbed a quick sandwich before checking his information device. This time he learned about the infiltration of Russia by the Unholy Roman Empire. The Russians had been aware of it by the time Tchaikovsky's ballet *Swan Lake* premiered, only after they figured out what the war with Napoleon had been all about. Now post-Soviet Russia was busy regaining control over the mineral resources, which had fallen into the hands of the corporate oligarchy with the demise of the czars.

Though done not as obviously as France had, Russia joined other European nations as covert allies for the American Revolutionaries. Hiding behind her diplomats and foreign advisors, Catherine II got away with a position of armed neutrality, while continuing to supply the colonies with funds and supplies for their products. Peter the Great had openly met with William Penn during a visit to London. After corporate-sponsored monarchies took over France in time for the American Civil War, the Russian czar Alexander II stepped up its alliance with the struggling nation. He helped protect the Union from the foreign interests that sponsored the Confederacy.

The struggle for freedom extended beyond kingdoms. The real war belonged to realm of the various sorcerers, who possessed the various kingdoms in their deadly grip. Napoleon had flaunted the issue in the faces of the Russians. The impertinence permeated all of global psycho-spiritual culture. Tchaikovsky's ballet *Swan Lake* illustrated this realization, depicting the ravaged Russian soul groping for enlightenment, which happens when nothing can be done about worldly entrapments. Russian art focused on the realm of the soul, a region that somehow escaped detection by the oblivious puppeteers. Von Rothbart held captive the soul of Russia in Tchaikovsky's *Swan Lake*. Most of the populace had fallen for the seductive Black Swan depicted in the false French elegance of *War and Peace*, while failing to note Tolstoy's observation that everyone loves the French because the French love themselves. National self-love conflicted with the selfish interests of nationalism. During the American Civil War, the British demonized the leaders of the United States. Russia, and France. This measure proved fatal for the Russians.

Von Rothbart emerged in the guise of corporate-sponsored White Russians from Belarus, the site of some of the riches oil reserves in the world. Like the complex Federalist switches dotting American history, 'White Russia' originally referred to Imperial Russia, or the White Swan of the country's imprisoned soul. *Roth*, a common European word for 'red', denoted the European communists. They also were funded, in the same manner that the financial Rothbarts had funded both sides during the war with Napoleon. Because Napoleon had married the unholy remnants of the

Roman Empire, the spoils went to his wife's Serpentine family. During the twentieth century, 'red' became another word for communism, and Red Russians had corporate sponsors as well. Both Lenin and Stalin had Western ties, and Stalin (another word for 'steel'), had been home-grown in the worker revolts of Belarus, only to be later promoted by the same foreigners who had seized the reserves during the revolution. By the turn of the last century, the Hegelian dialectic hit Russian soil and ousted the last of the Slavic Dragon flyers, a simplistic tradition emanating from the days of Camelon, the authentic kingdom of the Camelot myth.

As consequence, it didn't surprise Joe to learn that the KGB headquarters had surfaced in White Russia, where Lee Harvey Oswald had sex with the Russian general's daughter, a follower of the Roman Orthodox-church and promoter of Armageddon. As in the French Revolution, the Illuminati had converted the Freemasons to their cause. Now the poisoned guild, which once protected workers from serfdom, became a hideous global network with the sudden rise of the KGB agents, who were endgamers. Endgamers---such as Reagan and Gorbachev, with their penchant for staging authentic Star Wars complete with global destruction---promoted Armageddon. True Serpentine vampires fed off obliterated souls, and their treacherous control of scarce world resources was the means to the end. When the Star Wars game developed into a planetary apocalypse, Carrie stepped in to reverse the outcome as best as she could. She had winged it.

According to the information gained through this evening's two-way tap, the next step involved communication with the souls trapped in the other dimensions. Joe decided to sleep on it. He changed his plans, however, and sent Gabriella a late-night e-mail. To his surprise, she responded immediately. Obviously she was still on his wavelength, which assured and comforted him. Joe invited her to accompany him on a hike at Montara Mountain this coming weekend. For various reasons, this particular spot in the Santa Cruz range attracted him.

Gabriella wrote: *Extraterrestrials there are mining the region for gold and garnet.*

Joe stared wide-eyed at her timely response. How did she know? He typed his reply. *Did you see Swan Lake ballet at the convention center last year? It had a timely arrival in San Francisco. The extraterrestrials represent our souls in another dimension, one that has existed since the inception of the planet. Now you tell me that they are planning to communicate with us?*

A minute or two later, Joe received Gabriella's e-mail. *No, I saw Swan Lake when you were away in Mexico. I was jealous when you saw it last year, so I caught it when it came to New York. I wanted to see it too, after you and the guys kept talking about it during lunch. One of my girlfriends works in the ticketing office as a volunteer. I know what you are talking about, Joey. I wasn't born yesterday. I have Aztec blood. These things I know at a deep level. Another friend told me that the extraterrestrials were ramping up. Everyone wants this Mayan calendar issue to work out. Yes, our extraterrestrial souls want to communicate with us.*

Joe laughed when he digested her response. Gabriella said so many things once a person stepped in her world. Then he typed: *Later. It's past my bedtime. I'll pick you up Saturday morning at seven. Deal?*

Joe shut down his laptop, choosing to soak in the tub before retiring for the night. As he reclined in the lavender-scented bath, it occurred to him that the next addition to his project would involve a garnet crystal for communication with extraterrestrials. He wondered whether he would be able to reach the entrapped souls, like the lovers of *Swan Lake*. Different versions of the ballet had similar tragic outcomes. In the original version, the evil sorcerer Von Rothbart drowned the White Swan Queen and her prince. Recent ballets entertained a more Romeo-and-Juliet approach, where the White Swan forgives the transgressions of the prince, who commits suicide after he pledges eternal love. Apparently she never forgave Von Rothbart, though Joe suspected that had something to do with the suicide. Both adaptations unite the lovers in apotheosis, though the recent versions promoted suicide with solicited eternal-love pledges. What type of forgiveness would elicit a suicide pact? Or was it a murderous mind-control adaptation? Who knew? This is why Joey did not spend too much time at the opera or ballet these days. The story lines easily became head trips.

Joe submerged further in the tub with his thoughts. It all seemed very complicated, and he had so much to learn. The accepted interpretation was that the White Swan had been freed by the princely pledge of eternal love. The existence of the lovers continued only in the beyond, where the cursed soul was freed from the animal body. Hopefully, the soul had embarked on a shaman's journey in the beyond, instead of oblivion. The Russians had adopted the swan as a symbol of their existence. Having visited the Moscow opera with friends, Joe had experienced firsthand the pure elegant pathos trapped in their continued repressed state. Western enterprise was not their answer, and most Russians understood this now, thanks to Napoleon's French invasion. Joe's Russian friends preferred borscht to McDonald's hamburgers. It served as a national statement. For Joe, it was simply a matter of healthy eating, but his food preferences thoroughly delighted the Russians. Someone had convinced them that all Westerners obsessively consumed hamburgers in the fast food form. Joe attributed it to Russia's misunderstanding of true wealth, which included health as well as freedom.

This vague revelation painfully struck chords in him. Joe absentmindedly splashed some water over his face for emotional relief, attempting to soak some insight into his consciousness. He had left Gabriella many times as she tangled with the seductive Black Swans of various machinations. Known as a straight-shooter, Joe found no other path for him. Though he might be on the quiet side and hated to publicly admit his higher, more refined nature, he was a goner for spiritual elegance. Now that Gabriella had decidedly introduced herself as his cohort, he felt suddenly vulnerable and confused.

Taking a deep breath, he saw through the confusion and embraced the pain of forgiveness. Then he had to account for her history of machinations, complete with unclear motives. This scared him. Maybe the fear pertained to his own self-esteem issue, but he never believed that Gabriella owed him an apology or an agreement to collaborate with him. Life represented a chance, not a given statement to take for granted. There were too many variables involved with living. However, perhaps a universal law stated that souls were obligated to honor those who loved them. He didn't want to think about it. Instead he submerged fully underwater, blowing bubbles over his head. Then he leapt out of the water like a flying fish until he sat firmly upright in his watery domain. Joe still didn't know what to think about this. Why couldn't they just kill Von Rothbart? Would the princess still be able to break the curse if she went after him, instead of playing hard-to-get with the prince? Human beings needed other human beings to love, at least in the end.

Joe realized, however, that his thoughts had manifested too soon. The interdimensional woman with the auburn hair appeared in his tub. This time she left her purple dress in the ethers.

"You have a wild and free heart," she told him. Her eyes stared languidly at him.

Joe melted inside, feeling his brain fuzz over. Time stood still. For a moment he tried to resist the rapid escape of his logic, but he surrendered after another thought occurred to him. "Where did you come from? Did you have a past in human existence?"

"Yes." She softly nodded. "I passed over when Julius Caesar's army burned Avalon, shortly before King Cole I created Camelon. Merry ol' Cole and I were lovers."

"Enough said," Joe told her, sinking down again in the water. He recalled the days of his youth when he once purposely submerged with all his submarines for a closer look. A second thought entered his dazed consciousness. "I want to imagine a place where women don't need to be inside a castle for protection," he told her. "I want to build it with every engineering bone in my body."

The woman with auburn hair leaned forward and kissed him. Then she faded into the haze of his conscious thoughts like an eternal light. A quieted serenity filled the air around him. She had found what she wanted. "Only in the castle of thy divine presence," he heard her say.

"Hey, that's a quote from Yoganada," he accused her, but she had already disappeared and could no longer be held accountable. She left him face-to-face with spiritual enlightenment without any reservation. Despite this, the woman continued to answer his thoughts. Joe considered it rather decent of her, but he could not discern her advice, which seemed amazingly short and specific.

Stay with the castle. Drop the yoga. It's not grounded enough for you. Practitioners are prone to head injuries.

Joe rubbed his head in agreement, though he didn't know why. His mental sphere still seemed hazy and too safely tucked in a heady flurry to be controlled by any other mind but his. In the afterglow of the auburn-haired woman, he was left with only instincts and a hint of intuition. Maybe it had something to do with being a straight-shooter. Then he remembered Gabriella's words about bringing in the divine feminine. He had left her that day. Now he wondered whether she understood how intimate he was with the divine feminine, something she had sought through him, and something he refused to give her. Preferring to leave a tender moment alone, Joe got out of the bath and went to bed. Immediately he lapsed in a deep, deep sleep.

Chapter Twenty-One

False goals are

A gamble

Reference Tune: *Lido Shuffle*

----Boz Scaggs

THE NEXT MORNING Joe received a phone call from Donna.

"We need help understanding how the Lemurians separated from the Santa Dragons," Donna began. "It has something to do with the Lost Boys."

Joe drummed his fingers on his desk as he pieced the story together. "The Santa Dragons rescued the Arctos children, but they didn't lift a finger to help the Lost Boys, even in Blue Luminary form," Joe said. "This is odd, because it is easier to transport a Blue Luminary than airlift a child, especially one who doesn't believe in Santa."

"If they had believed in themselves, then it wouldn't have been an issue."

"You're right."

"Originally, the Lemurians sponsored the Santa Dragons on the planet and taught them how to elevate their existence," Joe started. "They supported anyone who wanted to isolate themselves from Atlantis. However, the Santa Dragons negotiated with the Serpentines under the table, and the Lemurians realized this."

"The Lemurians never trusted the Atlantean experiment," Donna added. "The Serpentines had blown up their planet. That hurt."

"Something about their existence on Planet Mu limited their transition to Earth," Joe observed. "They had to elevate themselves."

"Carrie said they got stuck in the blue frequency of the rainbow colors," Donna continued. "They were pacifists, and their approach to problem-solving proved unbalanced. They wanted to be left alone to the expense of leaving their heads in the sand. This made them vulnerable."

"They had to change the vibration of their DNA," Joe continued. "The Serpentines exploited their weakness, and the attack came by surprise. They hadn't been paying attention to what went on in the universe around them."

"The Santa Dragons were not team players by nature," Donna said. "It may have been what drew the Santa Dragons to the Serpentines, though in the end it backfired. They destroyed their high-flying villages. Their homes floated in the air like dirigibles. They tethered to the forest five hundred yards below."

"Something about the levitation phenomenon appeared deceptive," Joe insisted.

"How's that?" Donna asked. "Traditionally, levitation is associated with spiritual enlightenment."

"Not quite," Joe answered. "Like the Lemurians, the Santa Dragons longed for their former celestial lifestyle. They flaunted this preference in the face of the planet's inhabitants, which irritated them. Many were still recovering from the galaxy attacks, which brought them to the planet initially. Their lifestyle sided with the enemy. This became their vulnerability with the Serpentines. They secretly longed for the old, intergalactic lifestyle, which seemed arrogant. When the Lemurians saw through this guise, they left to establish the first Dragon flyer bases with the northern European natives and Celtic Atlantean survivors."

"They prepared for war with the Serpentines, while the Santa Dragons pacified the Serpentines," Donna remarked. "What ever motivated them to run off with the Serpentines' experiments?"

"They wanted children who would adore them."

Donna chuckled. "Good luck with that one. Part of a child's development pertains to the process of individuation. Their job is to internally challenge the wisdom of the elders and define themselves with respect to their peers or litter mates. Sometimes cortical development isn't a pretty sight. Parenting is the one job where if you do it well you get fired."

"You're right. Adoring children are very boring," Joe mused.

"I know," Donna said. "Apparently, the Santa Dragons were junkies for entertainment. However, the one thing that my teenagers claimed would send them into therapy concerned the reduction of their stuffed-beanie babe population to twenty apiece. Besides being un-washable synthetics and allergens, the stuffed-beanie population-control issue taught the children about meaning in life, rather than accumulation and collection. Now they and their friends rank colleges according to carbon-footprint scales. As young adults, they're very mobile, and the ability to just take off and go depends on knowing what is important to them. Now that they've matured, they enjoy the renewal that comes with the seasonal reevaluation of their belongings. They inspire me to keep on track."

"Downsizing is a great life skill," Joe admitted. "Although the Santa Dragons wanted to live lightly, they didn't in reality. The gravity of the situation literally caught up with the Santa Dragons. Those from

Alpha Centauri brought in a more balanced perspective. The Lemurians incorporated this as well into the Dragon flying tradition."

"That's all I need to know," Donna interjected without revealing what she planned to do with the information. "I know when to stop and when to go beyond."

Joe listened carefully to Donna's words. Without pushing for more details, Joe told her that he wanted in on the deal, recalling how Gabriella had taught him to pursue something of value. Donna chuckled again, protesting that she didn't exactly know where she headed. She relied on instinct and intuition for the moment and would get back to him after she had arrived at some logical conclusions. Respecting Donna's need to formulate her ideas before overstepping limits, or worse, stepping on people's toes, Joe let her off the hook with her promise that she would contact him when she had arrived with a mission statement in more concrete terms.

After a shower, he went to the office. In the dim light of his lab, he saw darting blue light streak across the room. The hues faded within several minutes and Joe calmly walked over to check his computer screen. Noting Dorothy's absence, he sighed with relief and read the message displayed on the monitor. *Forget the white light and go for the silver strings*. Joe ran his fingers through his short dark hair. Alone in his thoughts, he took a deep breath and glanced in the direction of Gabriella's empty cubicle. The absence of light from the hallway indicated that the cubicle room remained vacant. He had passed by those arriving early for the day. The lights from their offices failed to illuminate his space. Without mentioning the message to anyone, Joe resumed his activities. Gabriella and other members of the company came and conducted their affairs as if nothing out of the usual had occurred.

Later in the evening, after Joe returned home from work, he received a call from Joan.

"It's codependency," Joan announced, continuing the thread of conversation that Joe had with Donna earlier in the day. Regardless, whether she knew how Donna processed the information, Joan avoided the topic completely. Focusing on her specialty, which pertained to health issues, she elaborated, "The Santa Dragons were a codependent bunch, always looking for the next opportunity and never really settling down with anything."

"Not all that glitters is gold," Joe chimed in. "Like pursuing the silver strings instead of following the white light."

"What?"

Joe told Joan about his experience with the blue lights in the computer room. The color strung along the room like the silver swirls surrounding the merpeople. Mentioning the message on the screen, he sought further elaboration from Joan.

"I sent the message," Joan admitted. "Somehow it got to your office, instead of your home address."

"Obviously, the delivery had assistance from the other side," Joe quipped, resting his feet on the desk. In the diminishing evening light, he recalled his experiences at the beach with the departed. Then he changed the subject, "The type of neurotransmitters involved in levitation apparently can be addictive. The alpha state is only one of the four major brain states, which include theta, delta, and beta. They all must be balanced for human efficacy and productivity. I did some research on this for the design of a microchip."

"At some point in time, the hypothalamus must be satiated," Joan added. The tone of her voice betrayed her perplexity at Joe's admission. Taking a deep breath, she relaxed any ensuing frustration in her manner and continued, "Otherwise the hole inside never gets filled. The Lemurians gave up their notion of a pure race and mated with non-Atlanteans, reinventing themselves as the Druids. The Santa Dragons kept gambling with their position, whereas the Lemurians drew on experience and regrouped."

"It's like taking the blue-silver bonds instead of being blinded by the white light," Joe surmised. Images of the war in the Pacific flashed in his head. He told Joan, "Soldiers in World War II were sent to die in the ocean battles. The white lights marked alien transports."

"Correct," Joan said. "I wanted to warn you before you got in too deep. It's a trap."

"My friend on the other side survived oblivion by tracing the silver tie to me."

"She obviously wanted to make that point," Joan commented.

"The Dragon flyer lore that the Lemurians cultivated became critical to survival on the planet," Joe reasoned. "The past is the key to the future. This is where we can start."

"Or at least end it for the night," Joan said with a soft laugh. "I need to rest and spend some time processing this information. Good night, Joe. Thanks, again."

Chapter Twenty-Two

Sometimes it is nice

To have something to

Say 'sorry' about

Reference Tune: *It's Been Awhile*

----Staind

"DO YOU EVER feel like you have overextended yourself?" Gabriella asked Joe when he sauntered into work the next morning.

Dripping with perspiration from his bicycle ride in the dry heat, Joe politely waved her off without answering her question. He placed his gear on the floor and walked away. Heading for the restroom down the corridor, he smiled slightly and escaped further inquiry.

She had seen him parking his ten-speed at the rack outside her office window. Gabriella waited for him to shower and change clothes. Meeting him at his workstation, Gabriella noticed that Joe seemed a little more preoccupied than usual this morning. Quietly attending to details, he continued to avoid her spying eyes.

After he had stowed his gear in a large desk drawer, Joe looked up at Gabriella. Quickly rolling the drawer shut, he kissed her cheek and confronted, "Don't look at me; I am just a jack-of-trades. The entire planet is overextended. We're all over a barrel for oil at some level or another."

"I figured as much, Joey," Gabriella succinctly replied, savoring the moist peck on her skin. Satisfied with his answer, she lightly smacked her lips. Excitedly, she swiveled her chair around for another perspective. Gazing out the window as the dawn cast rays of pink light over the sleepy town, she decided, "I want to know more."

"I'm setting limits."

"Oh, Joey, that's a good idea," she excitedly agreed. "*Bueno*."

"*Bueno*," Joe almost whispered.

Gabriella's eyes danced with delight at Joe's agreeable response. "Okay, Joey, how are you going to set some limits?"

"I'm going to frame in my project according to the five major DNA types," Joe answered, sitting down at his computer workstation to type. He was determined to change things for the better; even Gabriella's chatter could not undermine his efforts. If he could maintain his sense of purpose, while humoring Gabriella, then he could accomplish anything.

With her playful words, she continued to seriously entertained Joe. Gabriella looked over his shoulder to study the assembly language code on the screen. For an instant, Joe recalled her naked breast, touching him only a few mornings ago. Apparently Gabriella had forgotten, but he hadn't. Lingering in the updated sensation, Joe deeply inhaled her fragrance, which also hadn't changed since the night she slept next to him. Rather than lapse in a sigh, Joe intently focused on keeping up the momentum.

"I see, Joey." Gabriella nodded. "This is sophisticated work. I can understand the first three DNA types: the Gauds, Serpentines, and humans. I presume that the Gauds and the gods are the same. As in Greek, Roman, Norse, and Aztec mythology, they mixed with the humans, but you must tell me about the dragon DNA. Where did that come from? And the earth spirits,

Joey? I'm not familiar with the fairies, elves, and gnomes. Is that like the dwarves from *Snow White*?"

Joe gave Gabriella a hurried glance. The shining twinkle in her dark eyes soothed him. He relaxed his shoulders and nodded at her.

"The archetype of the spiritual-magical warrior relates to dragon blood," he said. "Yes, the dwarves also possess the earth-spirit DNA, but their reproduction involved pollination techniques to reproduce themselves."

"I see," Gabriella responded. "Tell me about the dragons. How did their DNA get into the warrior blood?"

"Dragon tears," Joe replied with a firm nod. "The warriors who could comfort their dragons received their DNA. Wiping the tears of a dragon transmitted the DNA to the warrior through the palms of their hands. The palms of a Dragon flyer were magnetized to fit their dragon so that they wouldn't fall off during flight. Superconductivity transmitted dragon DNA to the flyer. It formed a special type of bonding."

"Oh," Gabriella murmured, lightly twirling around on her feet. "This is wonderful. I'll let you go now, Joey. I must get back to work. *Mucho gracias*."

Out of the corner of his eye, Joe watched Gabriella dance out of the room.

Good thing she didn't stay, he told himself with mild relief. Then he straightened in his chair, allowing his fantasies to dissipate. *Stay here, Joe. You have work to do. You can play with Gabriella later.*

Seconds after Gabriella left Joe, Dorothy Kilgallen appeared on his desk. "Back at work?" she asked him.

"More or less," he almost hummed, before searching the room for distractions.He thumbed through some of the files on his desk. Then he turned his head and gazed wistfully at his bicycling gear tucked away in a corner.

"You forgot about Diana," Dorothy mentioned, re-crossing her legs in front of him.

Joe ignored her innuendo. "Do you mean the goddess?"

"No, the princess," she corrected.

"Wasn't she after your time?" he pointedly asked her. He raised his head and looked around the room. The assortment of wires and electronics hardware contrasted sharply with the image of a princess and her accoutrements.

"Yes, but it related to the JFK assassination and the others, including Lincoln's," Dorothy said ruefully, puzzling over the connection.

"Same people?" Joe guessed.

"Almost."

"What does Lincoln have to do with Princess Diana?"

"They refused allegiances with Crusaders and Muslims," Dorothy told him, "which gave the East India Trading Company another reason to assassinate him. Like Francis of Assisi, he resisted the Crusaders and the United India startup companies. As a derivative of Constantinople, the Ottoman Empire owned both the Indian and British empires. Lincoln and Princess Diana intended to expose the fallacy of this religious war. The father of Princess Diana's lover ran arms for the Muslims. He waged his own little war against the British corporations, which worshipped the Indian empires. Even the name of his fabulous dress shop served as a two-thousand-year old political statement. He kept the name Harrods."

"Hmmm," Joe responded as he rose from his chair to retrieve a blank compact disc from a shelf. "A friend of my father told me about the

Ottoman War. When the allied troops reached the Muslim army at the top of the mountain, their own military leaders slaughtered them. After most of the infantry was dead, the allied commanders enthusiastically shook hands with the Muslim heads of state. As in the Napoleonic Wars, the *nadas* held the puppet strings on both sides."

"Money talks," Dorothy affirmed.

Joe glanced sideways in her direction as he resumed his work. "The same bankers who funded Napoleon and Russia opposed Lincoln for the presidency. After they poisoned his biological mother, he knew he could never play their game. He also knew they funded both sides of the Civil War. Somebody had to stand up to them. He had his reasons."

Returning to his computer, Joe pressed a few buttons and entered a few commands on the keyboard. He took a deep breath and continued, "Herod became a popular name two thousand years ago. Some Herods---like Herod the Great and Herod Antipas---were co-conspirators with the Jewish cause against the Serpentine Romans. Another Herod from the House of Judea, Herod Agrippa, served as a traitor. It gets confusing. Princess Diana didn't know her true enemies and never understood the significance of this ancient religious war. It involved more than just corporate greed and money. The textile trade has been intimately linked with the Crusades for a very long time."

On this last note, Dorothy began to fade from Joe's view. He didn't ask her to remain. Many hours had passed over the course of the discussion, and it was getting late. Joe looked at the clock and realized that Gabriella had gone home for the evening. Absorbed in his thoughts, he had failed to get lunch or notice the passing daylight hours. There were more questions to answer in his mind. He decided to go home and pursue these issues. His instincts told him that the inter-dimensional woman from Avalon would satisfy his passion tonight. This burning deep longing within him compelled him to gather his things, and Joe began the bicycle trip back home at dusk.

Hurrying home, he sped down the near vacant streets as the streetlights erupted in golden hues. By the time he reached home, he was completely in the darkness. After dropping his gear beside the front door, he searched for the inter-dimensional woman with the auburn hair as he quickly prepared dinner. He found her hovering around his laptop at the workstation.

"What do you know about the roman goddess Diana?" he asked her.

"She's not really Roman," replied the inter-dimensional woman. "She gave them the slip. The goddess Diana really came from northern Africa."

Joe quieted and steadied his hands on the cucumber that he was slicing. He needed time to think about her words. According to mythology, Diana was the daughter of Jupiter, who communicated with the animals and the woods like a Druid.

"You're right," Joe confirmed. "The Druids took her in. They reeducated her after they saw what happened to their Norse gods."

The woman slowly stepped closer to Joe, who suddenly had stopped his activity to watch her advance. Her soft, flowing movements relaxed him. Something about her appearance seemed timeless and reassuring.

"All of the other major gods and goddesses, otherwise known as the Gauds, failed to become human beings," he observed. "They never successfully transitioned to the planet from the celestial realm."

The woman stood close to beside him and took his hand in hers. She added, "That is why Diana is so important. She seeded the Gaud DNA with the Noris and humans. The Noris were balanced according to Vedic principles and incorporated the DNA of the gnomes, fairies, elves, dwarves, and other earth spirits. King Alfred the Great also seeded the Gaud DNA. His father was Thor."

"What does Princess Diana have to do with the goddess Diana?" he asked the inter-dimensional woman.

"Princess Diana was on a mission or a hunt, in step with her goddess namesake," the woman explained as she gently rubbed Joe's forearm.

Joe faced the woman beside him and planted a warm kiss on her head, just above her right brow. With his gesture, she began to melt into the surroundings, leaving only a shimmer of light remained where she once stood. Joe noticed her diminishing presence, and didn't protest; he found that he felt satisfied with their encounter.

A ring from his cell phone interrupted dinner preparations. Joe checked his phone and noticed that the call was from Donna. He wondered whether she had formulated her mission yet.

"It's about a right to privacy, Joe," she told him, as if their previous conversation had never ended.

"No, it's not," he told her without a hint of a tease in his voice. "That wasn't Princess Diana's problem. The Spencers have been pursued by Serpentines since the demise of King Gawain's wife. An ancestor of the Spencers betrayed Avalon. Later, the Serpentines killed her as part of the cover-up. Gawain suspected her treason and still loved her."

"That's what I mean, Joe," Donna responded. "There are no rights to privacy."

"Bingo," Joe elatedly confirmed. "The captain of the pilgrims at Plymouth descended from Spencers."

"How do you know?" Donna questioned him.

"Joan told me. Her last name is Standish, remember?"

"Oh yes," Donna mused with a light chuckle. "The early colonists voiced little concerned about privacy, which proved counter-productive to survival. Compelled to work together, they found little privacy onboard the *Mayflower*. Newcomers to North America admired the free ways of the natives. It captured the imagination of those searching for freedom across the Atlantic."

Joe laughed. "Who would want to wear fig leaves once they finally make it back to the Garden of Eden? Many colonists considered the New World paramount to Eden. European philosophers became fascinated by the concept of natural rights.

"Even John Quincy Adams went skinny-dipping in the Potomac River."

Joe roared with delight at the though of a president streaking across the capitol grounds. "I don't know. I suppose it was one way to move legislation."

"Stop it," Donna demanded, as she laughed with tears streaming done her face. "The founding parents never would have thought to include a right to privacy in the bill of rights. It's a double-edge sword at the fundamental level. The fig leaves must have arrived with the post-Civil War industrialization, when there was sufficient corruption to hide. The nation lost its innocence during the Civil War."

"Whether she realized it or not, Princess Diana represented a chess piece in a violent history, which the Serpentines intended to move forward," Joe told her. "Powers behind the East India Trading Company persecuted the royalty that the pilgrims left behind in Britain."

"Are you referring to the *nadas* operating the spice trade?" Donna asked Joe.

"The one and the same."

"Aren't the *nadas* related to Al Qaeda, the terrorist group associated with the Taliban?" Donna pursued. "Rumor has it that the Taliban are the descendants of one of the lost tribes of Israel. They're called Sons of Joseph."

"Yes, the strife has lasted a very long time," Joe answered. "The Sons of Abraham are also known as Brahmins. Gollum, the fictional character from *Lord of the Rings*, suggests that they have British relations, which concerns the US Pentagon. In the US, they are known as Boston Brahmins. Sacred cows, known as brahmans affect British currency. During the intergalactic wars of ancient Egypt, some of Moses's tribes worshipped sacred bulls."

"Much has been lost in translation," reflected Donna. "Like the human race, for example."

"I agree," Joe said. "They are literally lost tribes."

"The American Civil War pitted brother against brother, whereas the American Revolution involved brahmins against brahmins," Donna commented. "The company patriots battled for a stake in the Garden of Eden, which they considered to be true wealth."

Chapter Twenty-Three

In my head there's a swirling ballerina

A whirling dervish, a Sufi

Like the one that danced

When I opened my jewelry box in second grade

She twirled over my treasures

With grace and elegance

She reminds me that joy and laughter

Heal the soul

Even in the dank boulevards of L.A.

Where blue jeans are fashionable

And the best dances are found hopping

Over the waves in the sand

Reference Tune: *Tiny Dancer*

----Elton John

EARLY THE NEXT evening, Joe called Joan after work. Still fresh from his labors, he had successfully managed to keep conversations with Gabriella light without overextending himself. Even Dorothy Kilgallen left him alone today, giving him space. Joe had a lot on his mind, which the others appreciated. His office mates always welcomed the resulting analysis.

"It all comes back to the missions," Joe told Joan. "Good and bad. Princess Diana supported a mission from the days of Francis of Assisi."

"Tell me about the princess's mission?" Joan asked.

"Her mission involved the restoration of integrity to the British throne, in manner consistent with her ancestor King Gawain," Joe answered. "The Roman Serpentines rewrote history and left the women out. They had a difficult time relating to women."

"The difficulties of the Roman writers don't surprise me," Joan confessed. "The goddess Diana bridged the world of the Gauds with the humans and balanced earth spirits, whereas Princess Diana joined the world of the Gauds with the magical-spiritual warrior tradition known as the Dragon flyers."

"Where does that leave us now?"

"We must deal with the thinly disguised slavery of the Californian missions. Princess Diana countered the actions of the Hegelian dialectic between the Middle East and corporate British Empire. The corporate British Empire is currently the remaining Serpentine base after the fall of Constantinople. The roman legions left behind by Constantine lasted longer than the transplants at Constantinople. They have tentacles on every continent and in almost every nation."

"It's another kind of octopus," Joe surmised.

"Princess Diana called attention to it. I don't think that she wanted her sons to embark on holy wars in Afghanistan. Having worked as an assistant at a nursery school, Diana appeared ahead of her time in understanding the importance of a nonviolent foundation."

"The corporate portion of US intelligence worked both sides of the equation. Mohamed Al-Fayed, with his arms deals, balanced the crusaders of the Roman Empire. Slavery has been a component of the Middle East long before Moses."

"What's the bigger intergalactic picture?" Joan proposed, refocusing their discussion to make it more productive.

"It goes back to the Philadelphia Experiment," Joe said. "There were five men who were missing in action from JFK's PT boat."

"The Serpentines owned the experiment. It served as ploy to attack the Earth spirits. These people were targeted for spiritual annihilation."

"There's more," Joe told her. "It has to do with your name."

"Oh, yes," Joan said with a sigh. "Unlike my namesake, I'm bringing the divine forward rather than some Serpentine-sponsored monarchy."

"There's more," Joe echoed, pushing her further. "You invoke the spiritual-wizard warrior archetype. It is like the goddess Diana, who astutely evaded the ego traps that ensnared the other Gauds. It took someone who specialized as a hunter, someone intimately aware of the dynamics of the animal kingdom. Then she spiritualized it to the human dimension, becoming the moon goddess and the patron of childbirth."

Joan laughed with a sense of relief. "Diana, my hero."

Joe interrupted Joan before she got carried away and lost her feel for the seriousness of their discussion. "When I left for Mexico, Gabriella told me I was bringing in the divine feminine."

"I'm with you there. The divine feminine has been repressed for at least two thousand years. We don't know who we are anymore."

"Excluding fuzzy madonna imagery and all the many versions of Mary, the last time we saw the divine feminine was shortly before Camelon," Joe said. "Julius Caesar exterminated the divine feminine as part of his attack on northwestern Europe. Some men just carry women in their arms or sling them over their shoulder as a fireman's carry, but Caesar brought his woman home to Rome in chains. He publicly humiliated Cleopatra there."

"I'm not sure I'd call that love. No wonder Cleo ran off with Marc Antony, Caesar's enemy." Joan said. "I sense that the Diana archetype is a major piece of the puzzle, much like the princess archetype."

"I agree," Joe said. "I have more work to do. Let me think this over. I'll call later."

"Yeah, I need some more time too."

After Joe hung up the phone, the inter-dimensional woman appeared in front of him. She hadn't wasted any time in seeking him. Joe looked at her with a million questions in his eyes. Instead of voicing any of them, he lovingly embraced her.

"You need to protect yourself," he told her when he released his hold.

"Without reliance on a castle for security," she insisted, before drifting away with one final point. As she disappeared into the atmosphere around him, Joe sensed the silent echo of her lingering statement, "I want to live freely."

Her words ran through his head as he rushed to answer another call on his landline. Given the spontaneity of the circumstances, Joe curiously sought the identity of the caller. Discovering that Carrie had placed the timely call, he picked up the receiver and eagerly listened to the next phrase hanging on the horizon.

"I never became a big fan of Peter Rabbit," Carrie admitted without bothering to waste time with a conventional greeting. She had been tracking Joe's conversations with Donna and Joan. Wishing to get to the bottom line before she forgot the reasons for her call, she pushed Joe at breathtaking speed.

"What does Peter have to do with the divine feminine?" Joe asked, feeling bewildered by her statement.

"Everything," Carrie told him. "I never came to appreciate Peter until I had small children of my own and started drinking chamomile tea with Donna. I reinvented a proactive version of the story. Peter's mother gives him chamomile tea to help him recover from his adventures. Donna and I had a motto that we shared, *Parenthood, not just another job; it's an adventure.* I planted chamomile in the yard, swung the front door open wide for the toddlers, and told them to go forage. I taught them how to thrive under adverse circumstances, and I programmed them with 'be safe,' requesting that they never embarrass their parents by doing something stupid. When they were young teens, I sent them on a hike in the snow-dusted Cascades with a wilderness group, and they went with nothing more than a wool blanket. The oldest returned saying that he actually *learned* something. Two years later, he was hurrying out of high school classes to rescue people in the mountains. Eventually, the youngest became president of the teenage search-and-rescue squad. Now she's an EMT standby while studying at college."

"How? What?" Joe asked, fascinated by her conclusions.

Carrie explained, "Unlike Donna, I became more desperate and found away to escape. Today, the notion of running away remains the furthest from my youngsters' minds. My children, however, appreciated the experience of learning how to not just survive but also thrive in the classroom and out of the classroom. During lockdowns at their high school, I told them to tag with the teachers, who practiced martial arts." She further elaborated, "I don't recall the exact words, but Peter's mother admonishes him never to venture outdoors. It's a scare tactic, which I'm sure resonated with Beatrix Potter, who desperately pushed for a life outside of her restricted place in society. As a woman, she didn't have many other options, so she created them through her books."

"You're right," Joe said with a sigh. "Potter invested the earnings from her books in the exact places that Peter's mother told her little bunny not to go---the big outdoors, including gardens, rolling hills, and farms. That's probably how she accomplished her purpose under the establishment's radar."

"The divine feminine cannot be contained," Carrie continued. "All of my younger sisters ran away. My mother finally gave up and simply said we had the 'adventure gene,' but that doesn't really explain the longing and pain we felt on the inside. My youngest sister ran away at sixteen, and took the guitar that I had given her. She used the guitar to pay her way, until she returned home months later. We never understood the violence that we ran from."

"You're not into castles either?" Joe checked.

"Only as a reflection of inner joy and fortitude. Castles represent the value of refuge. Even gardens are contained; it takes savvy to thrive in the wild, which tests the strength of community and family relationships. In the freezing cold, people sleep together for warmth, instead of sex. The social mores change according to the environment, but the individual must learn to read his or her surroundings."

"And *deal*," Joe acknowledged.

"Yes, being able to *deal* requires self-discipline as well as a sense of the divine or an inner castle," Carrie reminded him.

On that final inspirational note, Carrie and Joe ended their call. They both appreciated brevity. Shortly after placing the receiver down, Joe picked it up again and dialed Joan. Of everyone he knew, Joan proved the most adept at navigating the multi-dimensions of life.

"How do you celebrate the winter holidays?" Joe asked her, though he wondered where he was going with the question. For the moment, he allowed his instincts and curiosity to lead. The breakdown of the Santa delusion bothered him, and he sought a more meaningful paradigm.

"We have a series of different family traditions," she began. "There are no sacred cows in our celebrations. First, we bake and decorate Christmas cookies with the gingerbread recipe from Michie tavern, a historic site below the hill where Monticello sits. When the kids were in their teens, they made them with their friends. During the kids' teenage years the gingerbread men and women bordered on the erotic, and their friends appreciated the cookies as gifts. Now the gingerbread cookies have become a tradition for us, one that takes up space on the kitchen counter for several days. We just cook around the cookie display as visitors come to check them out."

After pausing a few seconds to recollect, Joan continued. "Once the children arrived, we let them naturally gravitate to the celebration of their choosing. Like the oldest child, we arrived at the family traditions by surprise. I had taken the children to an elaborate puppet show with their toddler group. The show was about Babar and Father Christmas, in which Babar, an elephant from India, meets Father Christmas and a spaceship. The fact that Father Christmas gave Babar a decorated Christmas tree on Christmas Day impressed the children. Later, the youngsters informed us that this is how we should celebrate Christmas Day. So of course we had to comply with their sincere fantasy, much to our parental chagrin. It was difficult waiting for them to go to bed on Christmas Eve so we could finally roll in the tree and decorate it in the wee hours of the night. As parents we really missed not seeing a Christmas tree on Christmas Eve."

Joan stopped for a moment, before ruefully continuing, "So the next year, I elaborated on the Babar story, and as a result, the family decorated the Christmas tree around solstice. I omitted the Babar and Father Christmas puppet show in favor of an endangered species zoo with Santa and real-live hairy reindeer. They don't shave the reindeer at the zoo during winter, and this particular zoo has reindeer there all year long, which really impressed the toddler group that year. I knew I had pulled it off when I overheard my oldest child wistfully stare into the starry sky during the drive home and say thoughtfully, "This probably is the real Santa." Hearing those words made my Christmas that year. Positive illusions inspire me to absorb higher truths."

"By the next year, our toddler group proclaimed that we would start celebrating all the winter holidays, including Hanukah, Quanza, and Boxing Day. Larry threw in La Posada, because he spent a lot time in the Southwest. He hangs Taoist-style wise men on the tree as he traditionally begins the decorating spree by blasting Manhiem Steamroller. That's the cue for everyone to start decorating or miss out on the action. I usually shake maracas and leap around the living room, while the others sort out the LED lights. I guess it might substitute for a shaman dance, but I think my moves are more Native American. I'm a Leo, and if I'm not pouncing and roaring, people aren't happy. Eventually, I put down the maracas and start helping out. We top our tree with an elf. We're not very formal, and usually everyone votes on take-out Thai for Christmas dinner. There's a larger family turnout with this menu. We get the Thai at a favorite restaurant on Christmas Eve and keep it in the fridge overnight."

"Are you serious?" Joe asked. "What about the sacred?"

"I got that in during another year," Joan replied. "Eventually the children figured out the gift thing and rushed to open up presents early one

Christmas morning. I balked. When I was growing up, the first thing we did on Christmas was go outside. Houses were small back then, and the average adult took an hour longer to rise than my cousins and siblings. There's nothing more sacred to an adult than early-morning peace and quiet. So we went outside, and I learned that there is nothing more sacred than to be outside playing football with my cousins on Christmas morning. Playing just seems lighter. Anyway, I walked out and left the rest of the family around their gifts. Their burgeoning commercial ways really got to me, so I went Nordic skiing in the mountain cathedrals. My cousins lived far away by then."

"Did you go alone?" Joe quizzed her.

"Yes, I left them bawling with their little fingers stuck on the wrapped presents," Joan admitted. "They learned and came with me the next year. Being outside became another tradition. Later they joined a search-and-rescue group with Carrie's teenagers and spent more time outdoors. They'd grab some gingerbread cookies and tell me, "See ya mom. We're off on a mission. Someone's lost in the mountains. We might be back around three tomorrow morning." Life becomes more sacred. It's the ongoing process of discovering what's important, which sometimes only appears with the insight gained through downsizing. Now the gift exchange is more likely to be music, gift cards for camping gear, and warm clothes.

"Sounds familiar," Joe remarked, recalling his previous conversation with Carrie. "What do you do for Hanukah?"

"We moved it to New Year's eve, because we want start the year with as much divine Light as possible. We light a series of chakra candles, which also represent the colors of the rainbow. The intention is to move the light forward in an emotionally balanced way toward the future. This tradition helps put closure on the old year. It's a done deal with no regrets."

"What about Advent? Wasn't Larry raised Catholic?" Joe asked, curiously waiting for Joan's commentary.

"I bought a December calendar from a mother in the toddler group. The mother made the felt calendar with her children. The design is a Christmas tree with vacancies for twenty-five ornaments. Why only mark the four Sundays prior to Christmas? All the days before the celebration are special. Let's go for them all! The children spent so much time studying the calendar that even the cats wanted a piece of the action. When the children weren't looking, the cats would dive-bomb the tree and seize the ornaments. Then it became another Easter egg hunt looking for the stolen collections, which were in the cats' hiding places. It was like tracking the lair of a dragon; there was a trail to follow. We eventually eke it out every year."

"Fascinating," Joe told her. Does your family sing holiday carols?"

"Never. Carols lie in the jurisdiction of the compact discs. Sometimes Larry breaks out his guitar and sings a few pop numbers. The children---who have a piano, violin, harp, and guitar between them---usually erupt into a musical version of Reagan's star wars and compete for airtime. They enjoy performing theme songs from movies. After about fifteen minutes of discordant notes with *pluck, pluck* versus *sriwijng, sritwring*, the children start playing and singing together. Miraculous melodies fill the home. It's like hearing the animals talk on Christmas Day or something. When they go off to college, they carry three string-instruments in the car. The joys of the winter holidays land in the following seasons like snowflakes. Consequently, it becomes important to do Christmas correctly, though you never know what's going to happen."

"Sounds like it," Joe commented, cocking his right ear with a new idea. "I'll bring the frequency of seasonal celebration into my project. This final component is a big deal, on many levels."

Chapter Twenty-Four

No references

AFTER THE HOLIDAYS, Joe raced back to the office to research related topics. Dorothy waited for him near his desk. For the first time, he greeted her with a smile. Bowing his head, he studied his notes and asked her, "Why aren't you a ghost? You certainly haunt me enough."

Dorothy grinned. "I may not be as evolved as your Avalon queen, but I am here on my own merit, rather than trauma or drama." She crossed her legs and assumed a more business air.

Joe looked at her. Placing his hands on his hips, he fathomed the depths of experience behind the apparition. A thought crossed his countenance and he turned away to type more lines on his device. "You and the others are here because we need help from the other side."

"Yes," she said softly, nodding her head after a small gulp.

"Thank you," Joe replied, still typing away without a glance in her direction. He shuffled a few papers around until he found his answer, then he stared intently at the computer screen. "What does Alemanni mean?"

"All men," she told him. "They served as the male counterpart to Avalon, in a sense."

Joe turned around and blinked at her. "It's not fair that Avalon gets all the credit."

Dorothy merely smiled at him and faded from view.

After glancing at his watch, Joe quickly rose and donned a suit coat. He jiggled his keys in one hand and exited the building. Finding his car in the lot, he opened the door and slipped inside. As he considered the implications of a masculine Avalon, Joe drove through traffic to a meeting with a prospective client. Called Unite Electro, Inc., the company intended to hire Joe's firm to design an interface for their system. Joe parked in the lot beside a high rise of metal and glass. The morning sun reflected off the tower and almost blinded him. Shading his eyes to avoid the glare, he studied the manicured, verdant lawns surrounding offices. After collecting his soft, black case from the vehicle, he confidently sniffed the leather like a cowboy settling in his saddle for a rough ride. Joe strolled into the lobby and spoke to the officer at the security desk. Some gentlemen appeared from the indoor garden and introduced themselves. Joe shook their hands and followed them to the conference room where the director waited.

Sitting down in the arms of a concave swivel chair, Joe listened attentively as the director explained their situation. When he finished, Joe removed his proposal from his satchel and displayed it on the table. Without saying a word, he gestured toward the document and slid it across to the director. As several people studied the offering, Joe turned aside and thoughtfully gazed out the window at his car parked below with the others. Several vans from an internet company lined the curb. He watched several electricians unload a van and carry spools of wire inside. Joe searched the room for decor and motifs. Plainly furnished, the contents failed to describe the company. The pens and notepads lacked the typical letterheads and iconic messages. Joe noticed the director staring at him and looked at the balding man in the eye. Having removed any trace of curiosity from his expression, Joe sought questions from him. His response reassured the director, who looked down at the table and almost apologized. Instead he moved a paper form his side and pushed it toward Joe for his signature. Joe whipped out his own pen and listened as he signed. Within moments, he reentered the parking lot and paused to savor the environmental warmth of a climate not on thermal control. A hint of a salty breeze flared his nostrils as he turned his back on the sun-streaked building. He raced to his car and drove away from the assortment of phallic symbols dominating the horizon.

Back at the office, he sought inspiration from Dorothy. She sat at her usual place near his workstation. "It's a whole 'nother world."

Lulled by the presence of the spirit in the room, Joe softly communicated his thoughts, "I imagine that the Alemanni felt secure enough to avoid the artificial display of power through phallic symbols."

"Real men don't isolate themselves in steel, glass towers, or haunt coliseums."

"They play." Exchanging his dress pants for blue jeans, Joe deposited the contract on the desk of an absent co-partner. He called to Dorothy, "I'm heading for the beach."

Heads in the office looked up as he passed by and exited through the glass door in front. They watched Joe load his car and back out of the parking space. Sunglasses on, he looked forward without a wave to the onlookers. Joe tightly swerved out of the lot and waited patiently for traffic to clear before turning left onto the street.

Turning on the CD player to his favorite tunes, he rested comfortably in his seat and drove toward the sunset. He parked his car at the top of a bluff and surfed barefoot down the hillside on tiny grains of quartz crystals. A cloud of dirt followed him and rose only as high as his knees. At the bottom of the slide, he raced toward the foaming waves without stopping. The water rolled toward him and enveloped his legs above the knees. Joe scooped some of the salty solution in his cupped hands, splashing his face. Translucent drops trickled down his chin, and moistened his dress shirt in large splotches. The revival satisfied him and he turned around. Wrapping the wet dress-shirt around his torso, he headed ankle-deep down the coastline.

Several hours later, he inserted the key into the lock on his front door and entered in the dark. Sitting at a workstation near the kitchen, he saw Gabriella's silhouette outlined by the blue glow from the LED-computer screen. She barely acknowledged his arrival in the room. Instead she remained fixated on the information displayed. "Joey, all the money is electronically sent to a downtown hotel and beamed to a bank in India."

Leaning over her shoulder, Joe studied the photo of the bank in India. He mentioned, "It looks like the picture that Donna sent me from the geophysics lab." Straightening in his stance, Joe explained, "They mapped the location of the crystal skulls on Gondwanaland. The result depicted the world's eyeball on the universe."

"Interesting, Joey," Gabriella softly commented, still staring at the screen.

Joe sat down and rested in a nearby chair. He stretched his legs, before reclining with a yawn. "It reminds me of the search for the divine feminine with Donna, Joan, and Carrie. We uncovered the intergalactic conflict associated with the Mexican-American War."

Gabriella shut off the computer, leaving them both in the dark. Standing in the light of the moon streaming through an overhead window, she advised, "Say no more, Joey."

She rose and kissed him on the forehead. Joe blinked, staying motionless in the chair, while she headed down the hall to the bedroom. After glancing in her direction, he returned his focus to the moonlight and silenced computer. Within minutes, an array of sparkling, colored dots swirled into a recognizable form.

"Remember what Tobias told you," the multidimensional woman instructed. "During Abraham Lincoln's time, the slave trade extended from Havanna, Illinois to Havanna, Cuba."

Joe squirmed uncomfortably in his seat as he recalled the conversation with Tobias. Senator Calhoun, the former namesake of Springfield, Illinois, wanted to bring Cuba in the United States as a slave state. President Polk attempted to buy Cuba from the Spanish government in 1948, but the Cuban insurrection and Zachary Taylor countered the initiative. Patriots from the United India Company fueled the rebellion, which stoked the rising embers of the Confederacy. Though Jefferson Davis and Robert Lee declined to fund the Cuban army of filibusters, the slave traders procured support. Finding the extensive network of slave plantations unattractive, Abraham Lincoln defended the execution of the filibuster army, which included relations of the attorney general for Millard Filmore. Lincoln condemned the South's support of the filibusters. Years later, the company patriots successfully aided Castro in resuming the filibuster with funding from a former Cuban president called Socarras. Several members of the filibuster took photos in Dealey Plaza at the time of the assassination of the United States president.

"Yes, the face of the *nada's* bank in India does resemble the eye on the back of the US dollar," the multidimensional woman mentioned.

"When are they going to change that?" Joe asked.

"Sam Houston tried, but the filibusters ousted him. They seized Texas and put up their lone star flag."

"So Texas has the same flag as Cuba?"

The multidimensional woman only smirked in reply and Joe changed the subject. "Let me guess. After the Cuban missile crisis ended, Castro put Lincoln's statue in his Museum of the Revolution. Interesting turn in world history."

"Yes, the company patriots were not happy about the severance."

"So, *Guantamera* is authentic."

"Sincero. The Hispanics equate the terrain with the divine feminine, according to the song."

"How about singing *This Land Is Your Land* as they did to break the missile threat?"

"Joan knows how they targeted the musicians afterwards."

Joe rose from his chair. "I'm going to join Gabriella now. We have a lot of work to do tomorrow."

Chapter Twenty-Five

JOE FELL ASLEEP watching a moonbeam illuminate the opposite wall of the room. In his dream, he passed through a verdant forest where the rays of the sun trickled through the light-green canopy. The sun rays casted sparkles over the flowers blooming on various shrubs and plants. Extending her hand, the multidimensional woman beckoned Joe to follow her through the waist-high understory. Slowly, he walked toward her while he parted the brush with his steps. Distracted by the star-lit fairies interacting with the plant devas and elves, Joe bobbed his head up and down tracking the glittery streaks. When she turned around, Joe hastened to keep pace with her swift movements across the forest floor.

"This is how Avalon appeared in the beginning, before the fairies needed to hide," she said.

Joe didn't respond. Instead he paused, savoring the moment long enough to remember at will. He blinked at the woman when she glanced at him.

"I am taking you to Bilbo," she explained, continuing her journey. "You must remember what it is like to be here, so that you can find it again."

"I won't forget," Joe promised. "A person can't forget a place as wonderful as this."

"Yes, this where you can find your soul, when the rest of the world goes to Hades."

Joe grimaced slightly and studied the ground. Velvet grass only provided a hint of the trail's existence, which led from one vapor cloud to another. Like a frog hopping on lily pads to get across a stilled stream, Joe brightly strolled through the woods and gathered momentum with every step.

"Who's Bilbo?" he asked.

"The only surviving hauflin. He barely escaped the attack on the MidEarth as the American Medical clergy came to power and persecuted the defenders."

"Long story," Joe remarked without further elaboration. With a decisive wave of his hand, he signaled the end of the discussion as he moved forward.

"You're not ready to deal with the devastation, so we are making the passage in a dream state."

Joe quieted. A sense of calm shone in his countenance. The multidimensional woman stopped in the density of another swirling gray-white vapor and knocked on the door of a cottage. A man half Joe's height answered her call and closed the slim, wooden door behind him. Joe peered into the structure housing the hauflin, but only saw nothing.

"Ah Joe, what happened the last time that you fell into a light beam?" Bilbo questioned, puffing his chest in an assertive manner.

Transfixed by the juxtaposition of time and space, Joe straightened as he backed away a half step. Positioning himself firmly on the terrain, he paused a moment to recollect. He cocked his head from side to side and watched the vapor form spirals where the fairies had once danced. "I met a Hispanic woman from the 1850's. When I asked her about the children, she told me not to linger in the historic California mission."

"Why?" Bilbo questioned rhetorically.

The multidimensional woman nodded, crossing her slender arms over her chest. Joe noted her change in demeanor and shook his head. "She knew that their souls remained trapped in an evil scheme."

The multidimensional woman uncrossed her arms in response to Joe's answer. Joe looked at her briefly. Ignoring his stare, she waited for Bilbo to finish speaking. Joe returned his attention to Bilbo, who put his hands in his pockets and rocked gently on both feet.

"Joe, you need to hide," Bilbo instructed. "Make like a cloud and vaporize."

"Become formless," the woman added. "You are getting too close to what people don't what you to know."

"Like the entrapment of souls either through the legions of the Roman Empire, Spanish missions, or the American medical clergy."

"Canonization is for the cannons only," Bilbo continued.

Joe backed away from the encounter. Slipping into the void, Joe watched the others fade into the distance. He awoke early the next morning feeling refreshed. Gabriella had already gone into work and left a note for him in the kitchen. After a quick breakfast, Joe grabbed his gear and bicycled into work. He met the other coworkers in a makeshift conference room, comprised of several desks strewn together near some workstations.

Sitting down in one of the chairs, Joe told them, "Now that we have the contract, we need to hide."

"How's that?" one coworker questioned.

"Build the interface and make it formless."

"Like a cloud?" someone asked.

"It is either that or have the religious orthodox send your money to the Eye-in-the-Sky. We cannot trust United Electro.

"Sounds like a setup."

"We are selling off the building and creating a virtual reality company," Joe advised. "We'll meet at various destinations according to plan."

"Whew!" a coworker whistled as he sat back in his chair. Then he abruptly leaned forward and rose with two hands placed solidly on the table. "Next meeting is at the coffee shop on 47th Street. Bring design proposals. Meanwhile, I'll start packing, vacating, and selling."

The others followed his lead. Joe went to his electronics lab and began dismantling it. As he bent over an array near his desk, Gabriella came over and gently nuzzled his ear. Joe stopped for a moment to hear what she had to say.

"You must have put something to rest last night, Joey," she whispered absent-mindedly. Gabriella drifted away from him and gazed into space. Her eyes caught the sight of a coworker driving off and she looked out the window with a defined air of nostalgia. Turning on her heels, she offered one more comment, "You're free."

Joe looked up briefly and eyed her passage beyond the door's threshold. He heard the clatter of her footsteps from down the hall, followed by a dull thunder of a file drawer being rolled open. Several more drawers opened simultaneously as other coworkers dumped the contents with loud thumps. Remaining silent, Joe gingerly filled the carrier bags for his bicycle before riding home without a further word.

Instead of returning for another load, Joe deposited his bags at his workstation near the kitchen. After leaving a short note for Gabriella, he changed his clothes and drove to the beach. He bodysurfed in the cool waves and stretched his legs in a few frog kicks. Fighting the undertow, he didn't seem to go anywhere. Only his towel on the beach marked his slow drift down the coastline. Feeling refreshed from his swim, he left the water and walked back to pick up his belongings. For a moment he rested on his folded towel as he surveyed the horizon. The merpeople remained absent from view. No apparitions appeared from the foamy white crests to advise him.

At home, he found Gabriella's handwritten response to his departure. *Moving my workspace home where I can think. Meet me there for dinner at six this evening. Love, Gabriella.* Joe smiled when he read her message. He began rearranging his things in a spare bedroom to accommodate the items from the dismantled electronics lab. When the place began to look less like a gym and more like his former office, Dorothy emerged from the void and sat on a box designated for the new exercise section of the living room.

Glistening in the unlit room, she basked in the calm stillness of natural lighting from the window. With he head bowed over his things, she mentioned, "You ended a negative cycle. They won't be able to target you along with the other businesses and inhabitants of Silicon Valley."

Joe stopped and straightened before her. Meeting her eyes, he questioned, "What about the inhabitants?"

"When you go to the office, reexamine the wiring configuration with the internet and telephone."

Then she faded on him. Joe surveyed the wiring configuration in the room, which had been minimized to cut cost and detour hackers. Quickly, he cleared the space and hurried to the office after lunch. One of his coworkers greeted him at the reception area near the entrance.

"We already have a buyer for the property," the man told him. Covering the mouthpiece to avoid being overheard, he elaborated, "They want to raze the place and construct a high rise."

"They will raze the building whether we leave or not," Joe retorted, noting how the internet company linked the wires with an old TV cable and the latest utility innovations.

His coworker nodded his understanding. Immediately getting back to the caller, he said loudly, "I'll take a look at the purchase order this afternoon."

Then he firmly placed the receiver down and ended the discussion. Approaching Joe as he gathered the pieces of the electronics array, the man resumed the conversation, "They wanted to know why we were leaving. I told them that most of us had found jobs elsewhere."

"Our providers consider us an adversary rather than a client," Joe remarked. "When a telephone-internet provider ties the knot, they consider it a home-run for adding the service to the others on the block."

"We're playing hardball," his business partner surmised. With a sigh he left to finish packing.

Rushing to clear the building, Joe vacated the premises and carried his treasured equipment to the confines of his spare bedroom. He setup the workstation, intending to have it fully operational hours after he saw Gabriela. As he restored his electronics lab, he considered the new design for United Electro. The cloud would keep the money in the country in the event of an emergency.

Later, he rode his bicycle over to Gabriela's home. She greeted him at the door with a warm kiss. He hugged her and offered to help cut the bell peppers for a salad. As they diced the ingredients, Joe chatted about his plans for a fishpond in his backyard.

"I'll be spending more time there, so I want to make it more enjoyable. Maybe a frog will come and make tadpoles," he said.

Cocking her head to one side as she stared out the kitchen window, Gabriela remarked, "Joey, we're not playing hardball." Putting her knife down decisively on the counter, she washed her hands before garnering the edibles in a bowl. "We are evolving, like the dandelion eking its way out of the pavement. We will blossom with deep roots."

Chapter Twenty-Six

JOE TURNED TO face Gabriella as she spoke. Exchanging his glass of wine for a cup of green tea, he remarked, "Thank you for that feminine perspective. I'll drop my windup pitch for the next crack in the wall."

"No problem, Joey. I'll stick to a glass of wine."

Gabriella took another sip before stepping away to put the stir-fry in a dish. Joe filled a tray with utensils and readied the patio table for dinner. Sitting down, he waited for Gabriella to finish with last-minute details. A small toad leaped from behind one of the bushes. Joe rose to catch it, but the creature disappeared between the slats of the wooden fence. Gabriella arrived with another tray of food and Joe joined her at the table.

As he heaped spoonfuls of mixed vegetables and fish on his plate, Joe commented, "In light of the sobering reality, may I spend the night?"

Gabriella gulped her wine. Serving herself, she questioned, "Was it something I said, Joey?"

Ignoring her, Joe searched the vicinity for more leaping toads and wildlife. Not to be outdone, he pointed to a frog sitting in a shadow. "I need to catch some frogs for my new pond."

"Yes, I understand," Gabriella admitted as she affectionately touched Joe's hand. "No work for the weary."

"I want to be elusive," he confessed. Removing his napkin from his lap, Joe placed it on the table as he pushed his plate away. Instead of leaving her, he grinned softly as he partook her wine.

Gabriella looked down. Tears filled her eyes but none emerged from the ducts. She put her napkin on the table with an air of resolution. "We need to sleep on this."

Joe rose and helped Gabriella out of her chair. "We'll work it out in the bedroom. Go to the meeting at the coffeehouse and skype me in from my home."

Together they carried the perishables inside the house. The warm food went back into the unheated oven, whereas the salad items were returned to the refrigerator. The next morning, Joe awoke shortly before dawn and bicycled down vacant streets to his home office. Leaving before his departure, Gabriella raced back to the office to collect more items for the move and for the equipment to skype in Joe. This gave them several hours to make the mid-morning-meeting as productive as possible.

When Joe arrived home, he found a message on his answering machine from Joan. She advised him to protect the interface from orthodoxy. "It is what runs the phone companies. The spy networks are as old as the Vatican ratline of World War II."

Having overheard Joan's instructions, Dorothy popped in the reconfigured electronics lab. "Now you know why I always began with *What's my line?*"

"I take it that you didn't hang out with the dirty rats," Joe acknowledged as he continued making notes from the call.

"After what Hollywood collective learned about the Philadelphia Experiment and Kennedy's PT boat, we were all more cautious about the stories we created."

"So you prefaced your show with a line that would clue listeners in to the fish stories."

"I preferred it to Murrow's ending phrase, *Good Night and Good Luck.* My listeners were already strung out."

Pausing for a moment, she leaned over and studied Joe's scribbles. Admiring his mountain sketch, Dorothy became silent. "Tobias told me that Abraham Lincoln's real last name was Linkhorn, just like the Matterhorn. Now an old-fashioned horn serves as communication device, similar to the telephone and internet lines."

"So what did these mountainous horns communicate?"

Joe's smile grew into a wide grin. "Phone home."

"Is that the reason that a famous amusement park sports the Matterhorn and provides an Abraham Lincoln dummy?"

"If you wanted to hide a Linkhorn, you might relate a similar storyline."

"It covers up the truth about the American Revolution."

As a Linkhorn, Abraham's relations had been interned under the direction of a general fighting for the United company. They marched some of the refugees from the Battle of Lexington to stations overseen by the Transylvania Land Company. Other prisoners served on the shanghai ships or were sent to Australia.

Dorothy disappeared when the meeting began. One of the business partners displayed a schematic for the interface. He explained, "We need to block the lines stemming from Mount Pathos."

Far removed from the fascism and communism plaguing Europe and Asia, the headquarters for United Electro used orthodoxy measures to control the ratlines created in the aftermath of the First World War.

"That will be easy," Joe said. "The place excludes females and relies only on one side of the brain for perception. They have already limited their communication as a result. All it takes is one brain-infesting amoeba, possibly a microbe they created with their own endeavors, and the neural networks became useless."

"No evolution for these dinosaurs," Gabriella commented. "Hooray for the wild and free!"

The group continued discussing the design issues within the allotted hour. They dispersed to resume the transition from the building to offices and workstations scattered across town. Joe shut down the computer and returned to the beach.

This time, an apparition emerged from the white caps on the surf. His departed friend, Liz, came toward him. She stopped twenty feet away from his perch on a rocky seawall, where several gulls soared overhead. Liz pointed to a foamy outline left on the nearby beach. The receding waves left a shape that resembled the mountain that he had sketched in response to Joan's call. Immediately, he gleaned the information concerning Mount Pathos and the presumed underwater Atlantis. Liz nodded at him in affirmation.

"My company came next on their hit list," he murmured. Sighing with relief at having dealt with the latest round of targeting, Joe relaxed and reclined on the rocks. He closed his eyes and felt the wind blow across his face. The breeze lifted his previous troubles from his shoulders and warmed him with its scent from far away places, a gentle reminder of the paradox regarding constant change. The wind pursued another form of trade or commerce, carrying whatever wasn't securely attached. Joe reopened his eyes and found that Liz had vanished in the golden rays of the glaring sunset. With some minor reluctance, he rolled over to his side to gain footing on the jagged crevasse. Standing erect, he gazed at the Pacific Ocean for a few final moments and then drove home.

He labored late into the night to make his electronics lab fully operational. Without bothering to change his clothes, he fell asleep on a small couch in the room. The next morning, Joe awoke to the sound of the ringing telephone. Rising to answer the call, he sat on the edge of the couch and answered the extension.

"Good morning," Joan greeted in a cheery voice. "How's the transformation?"

"Transformation?" Joe echoed, cocking his head to one side. He blinked several times before responding. "What do you mean transformation?"

"It is not just about leaving the commercial office park to evade trouble or save your skin. It is about you finding your life."

"Like the metamorphosis of a frog?" Joe questioned, making himself more comfortable on the sofa.

"Tobias said that we can't just evolve; we must ascend," she answered. "You barely escaped with your life. It's a new beginning rather than the end."

He slumped back on the couch and considered her words. He observed, "The American medical clergy supports the company patriots."

"You mean the company parrots. Only the wannabes subscribe to the platitudes of the organization, which is not your friend, Joe."

"It's a thinly disguised pirate ship," Joe agreed, rubbing his head as if to erase any memory of past encounters. He stood beside the window and promised, "I'll call if I get into any more trouble. I'm still recovering from the shock of seeing the extent of the cruelty."

Having obtained his promise to call for assistance, Joan changed the topic. "Keep dismantling the Roman empires."

Joe took a deep breath and said, "Yeah, sure."

"The medical association of the time helped coverup the truth about the American Revolution. They faked Warren's death at Bunker Hill. The British company had to hide the bioterrorism, after having contaminated the wells. Most of those fighting in Lexington already had tuberculosis."

After the call ended, Joe checked his email. Gabriella and the group at the coffee shop had already submitted a proposal. Joe studied their design, appreciating the innovations. He replied to Gabriella's message about coming over to further explain their concepts. While he waited for her arrival, Joe added a schematic and several other components. He wanted the interface to accommodate other markets, breaking the destructive corporate oligarchy. Joe seized the initiative to create an interface that place the health of the planet at the top of the hierarchy, rather than corporation and unsustainable goals. The status quo rendered the nation vulnerable to back door attacks. Military medicine used Electromagnetic Frequencies (EMF) for its genocidal purposes. Traveling government officials prompted major cities to turn off traffic cameras, which could be used as guns. Political conventions often shut down broadcasting to sections of the country due to the potential for electronic foul play. Joe and his coworkers quit attending teleconferences for similar reasons. The EMF from a computer or cell phone could prove lethal. One coworker learned that standing in water broke the harmful radio waves from his cell phone while listening to a teleconference. Rather than miss the information, he chose to sit in a hot tub. Although this technique worked, he later declined to press his luck and attend another teleconference. Regardless whether the world realized it or not, everyone stood in the middle of what a researcher termed a scalar war.

As a teen, Joe learned about the radio waves blasting the Russian embassy. The television and newspaper headlined the event. As electronics became more pervasive in personal lives, the issue went underneath the radar while the entire world became more noxious. Initially Joe's company puzzled over this phenomenon. However, a conference in Las Vegas, home of every kind of trafficking known to humanity, gave them the full report.

"Just cross Donovan Way with Engineering Way, then you'll get there, one delegate explained as he opened a session.

The audience balked at his words. Wild Bill Donovan, brought the Office of Strategic Studies to the attention of US intelligence after signing the death warrant for Joseph Kennedy, Junior. John Kennedy's PT boat experiences, the Philadelphia Experiments, Tesla's thermal innovations indicated that the real war crossed enemy relationships. Given the historical context, Joe and his company wasted no time in disappearing from corporate-military view. Their next objective concerned interests of national security, which unfortunately Donovan had recreated in his own image. If Patton had been murdered to hide the evidence, then the electronic transfer of money to India supported a communist takeover, one wrought by the fascist-neocon hands that Donovan rescued from Nazis prisons. The Department of Justice had investigated many American families funding the Nazis. John Loftus wrote several books on their findings. Some family members went on to become US presidents and director of intelligence operations, and the activities continued for purposes of industrialization.

Knowing that some Russians today lauded Stalin's executions for the sake of progress, Joe and his company perceived both communists and fascists as unbalanced. During a business trip to Moscow, the tour bus showed them the marina where Stalin had shot five hundred members of his cabinet along with their family members. The place reminded him of Marina del Rey in Los Angeles. Unfortunately, the cabinet members lived in the same building and so the roundup had been easy. In the end, the Nazis had won. The vacated building in the present triumphantly sported a Mercedes-*falun gong* symbol on top, sorta like the high rises in Las Vegas. If the technology became lethal, then the investors would not live long enough to benefit. For Joe and his company, the mission to keep their money in the country pertained to a boundary issue and involved setting limits. For these reasons, they avoided politics and hoped that the communists and fascists would kill each other if they could get out of the way. Meanwhile, the company opted to take their loved ones and money with them, since they had never knowingly funded any communist or fascist.

For these reasons, the company treated Christians and Muslims as different sides of the same coin, bound for the misguided coffers of the ancient spice route resulting in the Crusades. They intended to impart value to their currency rather than entertain illusions. The company nourished the belief that Jesus Christ would have vetoed the notion of making human misery a commodity and selling it in the form of crosses. They argued that no human sacrifice seemed necessary for salvation.

Chapter Twenty-Seven

Intending to avoid the connection between US currency and underground trafficking sanctioned by authorities, Joe and his company became more productive as the quality of their life improved. No longer overindulgent, they scheduled the next meeting for the beach. Although there still remained a chance that Joe and his company might continue to be targeted for doing what they loved, they persevered and adopted tighter security measures.

"Hey man, where's your surfboard?" one co-worker questioned as he peered inside Joe's new white van.

With a wide grin, Joe looked up from his tinkering over the engine and offered to give his colleague a tour of the company's mobile electronics lab. Other coworkers entered the lot and parked around the vehicle. Slamming their car doors shut, they sauntered over. A stiff breeze ruffled the longer hair of some of the group members, and they scanned the horizon. Noting the persistent, jagged crashes of the surf pounding the coastline, one individual went back to his car for a hair band. After tying his hair back in a ponytail, he examined the configuration of wiring behind the van's dash.

"Nice set of wheels," he told Joe.

Joe remained silent for the moment as the rest fathomed the undertaking. A man with short, bushy hair climbed into the back as the wind blew his locks. Joe followed him inside and unfolded a bench seat. Handing him a document, he offered him a seat and a choice of beverage from the open cooler.

Thumbing his way through the pages of the document, the man waved Joe off. "Green tea for me."

Joe quietly pointed to the 12-volt hot water dispenser on the shelf. "Help yourself."

Other coworkers piled into the van and sat down. Serving themselves, they smiled lightly and glanced at the surroundings. An older fellow commented, "Reminds me of old times."

"Some things are worth bringing forward into the future," Joe piped. Nestled on a perch overlooking the gathering, he surveyed the expressions on those stretched on the pillows below.

"Surprise. Surprise," Gabriella announced as she joined the meeting. "Going 12-Volt gets rid of those nasty alternating currents. We spend less money on shielding our work from hackers."

The man with the wind-blown hair slapped the document down on the floor. Carpeted with a rug made from recycled soda pop bottles, the swift movement of paper remained noiseless. Rising from his seat with a grimace, he mentioned, "I approve. You'll get my design suggestions tomorrow via the email. Meanwhile, I'm checking out the waves to stretch out my legs."

Joe nodded. He watched the faces of the other men and women assembled. A woman looked over the shoulder of the man sitting next to her. After skimming the page with the diagram, she gazed at the wired equipment nested around Joe's position on the ledge.

"The LED technology minimizes power. The low power usage confines the electronic money transfers to local terrains, which means US, the United States."

"We just won't mention the LED components," the man next to her stated. He refolded and closed the document. Rolling the papers into a scroll, he handed it over to the woman. As she read the descriptions, the man remarked, "I'll check the email copy and send my comments tomorrow. The simplicity and mobility features are attractive."

"Beats the cubicle," another coworker added. "We can split whenever we wish."

Lingering in the van to chat and discuss the documents, the meeting reached its natural ebb. Another coworker drove the van home to make minor adjustments, and Joe caught a ride home with Gabriella. Following her inside her home, he filled his water bottle with water as Gabriella sat down at the counter.

"This will keep us out of the power towers," she commented.

"Maybe we'll reserve one for the holiday party," Joe said with a shrug. "Just a room with a view."

"I prefer keeping my feet on the ground, Joey," Gabriella insisted as she sipped a cup of chamomile tea. "If you want a view, take your mobile lab to the Grand Canyon."

"The air is fresher there," Joe observed. He rose from his chair and kissed her on the cheek. Then he left the kitchen to walk home.

"Do you want a ride to your place?" Gabriella asked before Joe closed the door behind him.

"No," he replied. "I need to think."

Stepping away from the porch, Joe took a deep breath. A eucalyptus tree across the street scented the air. Tobias had told him about the tree's antiviral properties and Joe's shoulders relaxed as he filled his lungs. Within two hours, he crossed over the threshold to his own pad and turned on the lights at his workstation. Noting that nothing had changed, he ignored the computer for once and checked his phone for messages. After listening to

Donna's voice on the recorder, Joe went to take a shower. Minutes later, he emerged clean and refreshed. Collecting his thoughts, he hesitated for a moment before dialing her number.

"Other countries want to use the electronic money during a takeover," she told him. "Keep it secure, Joe. De Gaulle defied world leaders by linking French currency to gold."

"My friends behind the veil tell me that President Kennedy wanted a stronger backing for the United States currency."

"I'm not sure that gold is the answer. You can't eat it."

"Yes, the currency needs to be backed with natural resources."

"I don't think genetically-modified-food is the answer."

"It's akin to fool's gold. Only those who want to go outer-space claim that it is good for you."

"In that case, they will never find life on Mars. The genetically-modified passengers won't have the correct amino acid sequence."

"Yes, life forms utilize only the left-handed amino acids. The right-handed synthetic forms are junked."

"Great. They can take the money and we can keep the food."

"It's a deal," Joe said before hanging up. Then he went to bed.

His company completed the interface several months later. Within a few days after the installation an armed shooter entered the same lobby where Joe had met the clients. Claiming to be a born-again Christian against gun control, the gunman exploded the building and the tower fell in its tracks.

To commiserate the loss, Joe and his company held their next meeting at the beach.

"There's nothing like food to ease the pangs of grief," one of his coworkers remarked as he heaped barbecued ribs on his plate.

"Here, have a beer to make it go down smooth," Joe added, handing over a cold, bottle of bitter.

Reading the label, the man nodded his consent and Joe unsnapped the cap for him. With a hearty sigh of relief, he brought the bottle to his lips and raised the bottom of the glass high in the air. Bringing the bottle down, he examined the contents again. He nodded as he cradled his plate in one arm. "Though the setting is a little rustic, the atmosphere sure beats the office."

Joe smiled softly as he watched the man join the picnic on the rocks. Grabbing a barbecue-chicken sandwich, Joe informed another coworker, "I'm going for a walk. I'll be back in an hour."

"Take your time," the man said as he dished a plate for Gabriella.

Pretending not to notice Joe, she conversed with the server about the different kinds of sauces available for the free-range organic chicken. Out of the corner of his eye, Joe saw Gabriella take her fare to a secluded log on the beach. The light breeze warmed Joe as he munched his food in the salty spray. A half-mile past the gathering, he noticed the silvery appearance of the merpeople sunning on the crest of the waves. When they saw him, they animatedly bounced in the surf.

"Lighten up," they communicated. "It's only a tower. It's not the world."

"True, it didn't come to that," Joe responded. He stopped his quick pace and sat down on a bluff near the water's edge. Hidden from view of the picnickers, he began doodling in the sand. Without looking up from his drawings, he silently told them that he had gained clarity from the experiences.

"Don't rock the boat," the merpeople advised.

"I'm too scared to rock anything."

"Expect positive results."

Joe looked up from his sketches and saw a coworker approach him. Older than the rest, he had been the first to approve the mobile electronics lab. The man with gray hair waved at Joe. With gestures, he asked whether he could join him. Giving up his solitude, Joe invited the elder over.

"Gabriella seems angry," he mentioned as he sat down next to Joe.

"She is," Joe offered. "She picked up on the targeting."

"So it wasn't the lone-nut pattern." Leaning back to recline, the elder stared at the horizon and remarked, "We all knew that.

"She is concerned that we all might be targeted," Joe added as he hurled a skipping stone at the receding tide. "They might come after us now that their ploy to hijack the money out of the country failed."

"Like the waves, we gotta roll with it," the elder remarked.

The two men stood and walked back to the van. Gabriella and some of the other coworkers had already left the scene. Joe secured the van before sliding into the driver's seat. With a light wave, he said acknowledged the departure of the elder in his vehicle. Joe followed him out of the lot, turning in the opposite direction.

Leaving the van in the garage, Joe entered the kitchen and met the multidimensional woman at the usual workstation.

"Any words of wisdom for those who are freaked?" he calmly asked her as he checked his emails and phone messages.

"Relax," she told him. "Stay detached from those pursuing a slippery slope."

"How do I know whether I'm on a slippery slope?"

"Keep hopping and calling for that next lily pad. Water carries sound."

Joe dialed Gabriella's number as multidimensional woman spoke. Without bothering to listen to Gabriella's message, he waited for her to answer his call. Recognizing his number, she got straight to the point.

"Joey, I think that it is time that we visit the Grand Canyon."

"I need water," he insisted.

"Hmm. Water carries sound. We could put the van on a ferry to one of the local islands."

"I'll be over in an hour," Joe agreed before ending the call. He glanced at the fading multidimensional woman. "I want you around for the leap."

"I'll be in the van," she promised with a subtle shimmer.

Joe loaded the van with his gear. He drove to Gabriella's house after texting his coworkers to 'play possum.' They cancelled meetings for the next two weeks and arranged to continue working in small groups. Joe and Gabriella caught the midnight ferry. Sighing with relief as the vehicle boarded the vessel, both of them looked at each other and nodded.

Chapter Twenty-Eight

On board the ferry, Joe left the parked van to walk around the deck and stretch his legs. Gabriella dozed inside the back of the vehicle. Touring the ferry as it sailed across the sea, Joe entered the refreshment area. A television positioned above the vending machines blared the latest news about the shooter's identity. The reports came from cell phone videos taken during the attack.

Throwing colorful, fluorescent, plastic crucifixes at his hostages, he promised to take them to heaven. "I'm saving your souls. The only way to get to heaven is to suffer. If you suffer long enough, you'll want it. Smile. God loves you."

Joe sighed and headed toward the exit. The womb-like darkness on the other side of the glass windows appeared soothing in comparison to the dark commentary. A janitor emptying the trash containers near the door nodded at Joe as before he passed through the threshold.

"As far as I know Jesus Christ never passed out crosses," he said with a wink. "Only Hitler and his Teutonic knights."

Joe briefly paused to gaze into the man's eyes. His calm manner assured Joe. Relaxing his shoulders, he glanced back at the news scene broadcasted on the elevated screen.

"My sponsors said that they would donate the funds to charity," the shooter rambled before the set went blank.

"Like the Blue Crosses given to mothers having the most Nazi babies," Joe softly responded.

The man straightened and stopped repacking the container with the liner. With a twinkle in his eye, he rejoined, "Some call it insurance."

"Well, I supposed if you want the care of an insane, homicidal dictator," Joe commented as he pushed open the glass door.

Wisps of fog laced the starry skies over Joe's head. A gentle, cool breeze raised the hairs on the back of his neck. Joe hurried back to the vehicle and hopped in the driver's seat. Refreshed from her nap, Gabriella climbed into the passenger seat.

"How's the activity on deck?" she asked.

"I met a time traveler," Joe answered, gazing at the luminous dials on the dashboard. He turned on the radio to a station that only played music. Setting the volume on low, he commented, "We're getting the divine help that we need.

Lights from the ferry lit the features on Gabriella's face. Joe watched her jaw become firm as her eyes glistened with tears. Her cheeks bore the marks of dried, salty streaks. She turned her head slightly and nodded at him.

Gazing at the dark horizon before the vehicle, Joe offered, "I learned long ago, while playing basketball against seminarians. Never play games with the sexually-frustrated."

"Is that why they go for the towers?"

"And why they erect them and sexualize pistols."

"If the shooter started out life with a circumcision, I can understand why he would want to be born again."

"Medical habits die hard."

"Obviously."

When the ferry docked, Joe drove the van over the ramp and merged onto the main street. He headed for a part of the island known for its shark and whale watching. Finding a vacant campground, Joe parked and secured the vehicle. Gabriella inflated a mattress and arranged it behind the front seats. They fell asleep on floor of the van.

In the morning, they roamed the beach while guarding the electronics lab inside the vehicle. After sending messages to their coworkers, they shared breakfast and counted their blessings. The serenity of the isolated campground contrasted sharply with the mayhem of the overseas cities. Gulls flew overhead as crickets and frogs sang at a nearby pond in the grove. As Gabriella made some minor changes to other projects, Joe hiked the wooded area to avoid being easily spotted on the beach. His coworkers informed him that the last-minute adjustments prevented their former building from exploding like those in surrounding neighborhoods. Joe returned to the van and relieved Gabriella from her watch, so that she could explore the rustic scenery.

As Joe checked his email, the multidimensional woman appeared beside him. Appreciating her assistance, he stopped and focused on the apparition.

"Dorothy is here, too," she communicated as the familiar form materialized on an electronics cabinet across the room.

"Hold your position," both said in unison. "Some of their plan backfired and they are regrouping. When the dust settles, you'll have a better picture of what to anticipate."

Joe glanced out the tiny porthole at the gray, turbulent waves pounding the surf. Only a few people remained, scattered in the campground about a quarter mile apart. In the echo of the melodious waves, Dorothy related the historical context. Apparently, Eden traded with the settlement on Iron Mountain. The progenitors of the human form, Adam and Eve enjoyed intergalactic contacts. The contacts communicated through the placement of crystal skulls. When Serpentines stole one of the Golden Apples in the celestial realm, they disturbed the crystal skull network on the planet. Then they destroyed the extraterrestrials operating the network. The Serpentines replaced the crystal skull network with the skull and bones of mortals. The femurs cross the calcified head of the human and mark the trade routes for planetary exploitation. Pirated goods become destined for outer space. Then a friend of the Chair of the United States Federal Reserve, a privately-owned company, wrote a book called *Fountainhead* that placed Iron Mountain elsewhere. As in the song *Sympathy for the Devil*, black appeared as white and white became black. According to clinical psychologists, such illusions seed schizophrenia because the individual is left to negotiate the split between good and evil.

"Why didn't you tell me that we were taking on godzilla?" Joe asked. He rose from the workstation to face them both.

"It became an inevitable destiny," the multidimensional woman replied.

"Comes with the planet," Dorothy piped.

"So what do I do now?" Joe questioned. Fumbling a dial with a hint of exasperation, he consulted his information device for an inspiration.

"Contact the pre-Eden base known as Iron Mountain," the multidimensional woman instructed. "Go back to that sea shell shop in town and find a nautilus shell. Tune to the frequency of that baffled structure."

Joe glanced at Dorothy for more contemporary insight. She merely nodded at him. Bowing her head, she deferred to the multidimensional woman.

"Iron Mountain secured their networks from the galactic pirates eons ago," the multidimensional woman continued.

Gabriella climbed into the back of the van and announced, "I heard the news, Joey. I'll bicycle into town for the nautilus shell. I can sense the whispers of the other women in the lab."

Seated at the workstation, Joe ignored Gabriella and peered out of the porthole window. A fog rolled over the waves, enveloping the campground in a gray, dewy mist. Without a clear demarcation between sky and sea, Gabriella appeared dazed from her stroll over the terrain.

"How will you see the road?" he asked in a concerned voice.

"I've noticed that there is greater visibility outside of the campground. I'll go slow," she told him as she retrieved her cycling gear. Turning away from Joe, she made it clear that she could not be stopped. "Keep the lines of communication open, Joey. I want all the help that I can get."

The fog lifted sometime in the wee hours of the night. By the next afternoon, Joe had configured the electronics lab and interface to the harmonics of the nautilus shell. Gabriella and Joe left the van for a walk on the beach. They held hands during their quick jaunt to the small, unfurling waves on the shore. Never straying away from a view of the vehicle, they waded in the cool water as Joe searched the horizon for sign of the merpeople. Noticing a few shapes in the distant surf, he communicated with them about the latest events, describing the detonation of explosives in the cities.

"Oh yes, intuitives fifty years ago foresaw the rebuilding of the major cities," the merpeople communicated. "It loomed as an inevitable destiny."

Sensing their inaudible discussion, Gabriella raised her head and surveyed the area. Joe watched the expression on her face relax as she found a voiceless understanding of the situation. Without blinking, she stared at the water's edge and commented, "I can tell that you have more silent friends here, Joey."

Without listening for his reply, she reached down to pry a sand dollar from the sand. Joe let go of her hand and stepped away. Looking down at her find, he told her, "Apparently, there is more to come. There's a prophesy to fulfill."

"I know, Joey. My grandmother's aunt told me once that I would live long enough to see the cities rebuilt."

Having overheard Gabriella's admission, the merpeople danced on the frothy waves with a silver shimmer. Joe politely bowed out of the quiet discussion, leaving Gabriella alone on the beach with the highlighted presence of the merpeople. He went to check his cell phone messages. Donna's voice on the recorder advised him to find another place to stay.

"Time to get lost on the mainland. Eli learned that there's a major shipping channel used by United Electro for imports. There's only one way off the island. If they decide to come looking for the interface, then you could be trapped."

Gabriella emerged in the back of the van. Dripping wet from the ocean spray, she removed her nylon jacket. She noticed Joe repacking the van. Without a word, she began readying the vehicle for departure.

"Until I get confirmation from Iron Mountain, I want to keep the interface under the radar," Joe explained. "Donna told me that they might sail by."

"Let's take it to my place, Joey," Gabriella suggested as she carried a box of gear to the front. "At my pad, the van surfaces as a romantic interlude. At your place, the van appears suspicious. They may not know much about us, Joey, but everyone knows that you are too pragmatic to keep a vehicle for the sake of courting."

"Engineers have a reputation that precedes them," Joe remarked with a smirk.

"Yes, but it is true," Gabriella insisted. "Let's not tempt fate."

Moments later, Joe reluctantly parked the van in Gabriella's garage. He sighed as he made notes about all the minor repairs to perform at his place. Then he slid out of the driver's seat and slammed the door tight. Meeting Gabriella in the kitchen, he unpacked and prepared lunch.

Nibbling on a few light snacks, they sorted through supplies. Nobody mentioned the next move. Instead they ran through the suggestions offered by their colleagues. Eventually, they agreed to leave the van at a mechanic's shop, via a friend of a friend of a friend.

Chapter Twenty-Nine

HAVING ANTICIPATED THE vulnerability of office buildings, the wisdom of moving electronics lab to a van proved invaluable. While other businesses went off track, Joe and his coworkers evolved. As a result, his company continued to served its clients despite the surrounding destruction. The auto repair shop increased its already tight security concerning vehicles left on the premises. Joe rode his bicycle and dressed like a mechanic before working in the van's electronics lab. Other coworkers did the same and the rapport with the shop's mechanics encouraged further innovations.

"What would a confirmation from Iron Mountain look like?" Joe asked Gabriella as they discussed the recent developments several days after returning from the island.

Looking up briefly from the carrots that she sliced on the counter, she shrugged. She turned away from Joe. The imagined weight on her shoulders conveyed a sense of hopelessness. Joe dropped the matter and they quietly shared dinner before he bicycled to his own place.

The next morning, he retrieved the mail from the box and found his answer. Almost mistaken for junk mail, he noticed an advertisement for lakeside cabin at Iron Mountain, Arkansas. Rather than pursue his inquiry with Gabriella, he called his friend, Tobias.

"I'm going," he told Tobias. "Would you and your wife care to share a cabin with me?"

"Yes," Tobias immediately decided. "The timing is amazing. Last week, Michelle traced her family tree to that area. I know she wants to check it out."

"We may have to look in another dimension once we arrive," Joe speculated.

"I know, but I also know that ninety percent of life is just showing up," Tobias responded. "Maybe your multidimensional woman can help us."

"I'll investigate that approach," Joe said, "If Gabriella doesn't come up with something first."

Over a late dinner, Joe broached the subject with Gabriella. As she took her first sip of red wine, he softly teased, "I have confirmation. Tobias, Michelle, and I leave for Iron Mountain in six months."

"That's nice, Joey," she said nonchalantly with a languid stare at the flickering candle in the middle of the table. Refusing to meet Joe's eyes, she informed him, "I have learned that there are no surprises with you, Joey. I'll stay and guard the van, while you play in other dimensions with your friends."

Still hesitating to look him in the eye, Gabriella rose from table. Taking her wine glass with her, she exchanged it for a glass of water. For a moment, Joe studied the rock designs in the countertop. He mentioned, "I figured as much. Tobias didn't even ask whether you'd join us, though he signed up Michelle without eliciting her direct consent." Leaving his nearly full wine glass on the table, he walked over to Gabriella. Touching her elbow gently, he requested, "Look at me."

She turned and brought the water to her lips, as she positioned the goblet between them. Tobias put his hands around her waist and pulled her closer until his kissed her forehead. Tears filled her eyes as she told him, "I don't want you to go. Can't we find salvation another way?"

"Don't think of it that way," he said. "I am here to celebrate."

"Then send me a postcard, Joey."

"Maybe."

"Gabriella, it's over," Joe told her as he backed away. His expression conveyed a sense of shock over his decisive words, which had emerged from the depths of his being. "I don't want to string you along, nor do I want to be strung along."

"I know," she said, turning away from him to stare at the mosaic in the countertop.

Having heard her reply, he headed for the front door. "I'll come tomorrow for my things when I bring your stuff."

Walking out in the fresh breeze, he spied a leaping toad from under a nearby brush. After the creature disappeared from view, he rode his bicycle home. Upon arrival, he checked his email at the workstation by the kitchen. Finding no messages, he turned on his heels and walked toward the spare room, which had become his in-home electronics lab. As he searched this room for anything in particular that belonged to Gabriella, the multidimensional woman appeared in a sunbeam emanating from the window.

"You now longer seem to be carrying a burden, Joe," she communicated as he surveyed the lab's contents.

"It happened so quickly," he commented.

"There's no time for second guessing. You made your move."

"And I am moving. I have six months to straighten everything out, then I leave for Iron Mountain."

"The moment will come quickly. There isn't anytime to spare in regret," she remarked as she faded from view.

Joe collected Gabriella's things and piled them on the bed in the next room. Satisfied that the process of disengagement had begun, he lit a green candle in the kitchen and savored a glass of sassafras tea. Taking his glass with him, he blew out the candle and walked outdoors. Sitting next to his pond, he watched the minnows dart between the shadows reflecting the nearby brush. He compared Gabriella's perspective to those of his own world. His ancestors had inhabited North America long before settlers carved out Connecticut. The Conn druids worked with the refugees crossing the Bering Strait. Together, they established beaten paths, which the Vikings haunted.

Joe bicycled to the auto shop and checked with the coworkers maintaining operations inside the van. He gave him notice that he would be taking an extended vacation in six months. Despite the change in appearances, the company's transformation yielded greater productivity and enthusiasm amongst the employees.

"Oh you're leaving us," an administrative clerk joshed.

"I'll be back," he promised. "If all goes well, we might have a more secure and robust company."

"We'll stay tuned," he said with a grin. As he glanced at the monitor in front of him, his expression grew serious. "You know, Joe, tragedies can bring people together, and other times it wedges them apart."

Joe stared at him. Without any further expression, the man simply winked and resumed his work. Joe bowed his head left the shop. At home, he started making arrangements for his trip to Iron Mountain. He emailed Tobias a copy of his reservations for the plane trip and cabin. Looking up from his work, he noticed the multidimensional woman standing near his desk. She sparkled in the diminishing hours of the daylight.

"Why are you here?" he asked. Confused by the apparition's sudden interruption, Joe reexamined his notes.

"CHOICES, Joe," she answered.

As she spoke, the phone rang. Joe implored her for further explanation, before responding. The number came from out-of-state, and Joe turned his focus to the caller.

"I'm the owner of the cabin resort at Iron Mountain," the man greeted. "We look forward to your arrival. Do you have any concerns or questions?"

"Yes, can I bill my company?"

"Sure. We'll switch it over. What's the number?"

When the transaction finished, Joe placed the receiver down and emailed Gabriella. He informed her that he intended to go to Iron Mountain on business. She emailed him back. *Good Joey, then we can still be friends. I'll help you pack.*

Joe rose from the workstation and went outside to listen to the creatures singing at his pond in the night. Slipping into his backyard unannounced, Gabriella pulled up a chair and sat down near him. Without a word, Joe waved in greeting. Together they relaxed in silence as the stars came out in the sky. After a half hour, Joe rose and offered to get her a glass of red wine.

"No thank you. I am too tired tonight."

Joe left her alone in the moonlight, later returning with a glass of champagne for himself. Sitting back down in his chair, he sipped the beverage in the streaks of moonbeams striking the turf. A slight breeze ruffled his short hair.

Breaking the silence again, Gabriella remarked, "You know, Joey, some flowers only open when the wind blows."

Joe smiled. "After having spent so much time lately at the beach, I am ready for the mountains."

Six months later, Joe boarded a plane bound for Arkansas. Glancing at his cell phone before turning it off, he read a text from Gabriella. *The system has already crashed. We are rebooting it now. This time we are taking the van to an amusement park. Love, Gabriella.*

Instead of responding, Joe complied with airline regulations and turned off his cell phone. When the plane landed in Arkansas, Tobias and his wife, Michelle, met him at the baggage claim. Everyone dressed casually in cotton shirts and blue jeans. With her long, dark hair flowing behind her, Michelle gave Joe a quick embrace. As they stepped outside together, a soft wind blew over the flat terrain. Tobias ran his fingers through his sandy-blonde hair, before beckoning Joe toward their vehicle. They helped him load his luggage in the car, before driving to the cabin resort.

"How's Gabriella doing?" Tobias asked.

Joe smirked and replied, "Oh, she's *dealing*."

Tobias glanced in his rearview mirror at Joe. "We'll send her a postcard."